Under a Blue Moon

Steve Higgs

This book is for the wonderful people that love books and have found me and my fun little world.

Contents

Day One. Thursday, March 18th 0545hrs

I HAD THE LOCAL newspaper in my hands. I had been staring at the advert on page forty-seven for at least five minutes because I couldn't work out what to do when I finished staring at it.

Sitting in my small office with its sparse decoration, my entire focus was on a single word in one line of text. It was a word in the title of the advert I had paid a local newspaper to run for my new private investigations business.

Upon seeing it for the first time five minutes ago, I had reacted with uncharacteristic panic as my heartrate spiked from the shock. As I had forced myself to calm down, my next task had been to check what I had submitted to the newspaper just in case I had suffered an aneurism when I wrote the text for the advert and the error I could now see was somehow my fault.

It wasn't.

Having confirmed the disaster was not of my own making, I picked up my phone and called the paper. When the line connected, I asked for the editor and was transferred to someone who was not the editor, got transferred again and finally reached someone I felt it was okay to shout at.

'Martin Coruthers. How may I help you?' I didn't know the editor so there was no relationship to leverage or damage, but it was a small, local paper that circulated to a readership of a few million and I knew the staff to be a small team thus the editor was a person that had sway over every element on every page. Unlike with a large national paper, he would be a person I could reach and deal with.

'Mr Coruthers. My name is Tempest Michaels. I paid to have a half page advertisement for my new business. I'm unhappy to report that you have misrepresented me.'

'How so?' he asked, his voice wary.

I was staying calm. Raising my voice would achieve nothing and make me appear less in control. 'I run a private investigation business, Mr Coruthers. Today is my first day of operation and I find my business erroneously advertised under the heading Paranormal Investigation.' He said nothing, 'Worse yet, the person that wrote the advert elected to use some artistic license, by which I mean they added a short poem.'

'A poem?' he echoed.

'Yes. A short verse or a ditty one might call it. Shall I read it to you?'

'Err, okay,' Mr Coruthers sounded resigned and a little dismayed as if this had perhaps happened before.

I paused before starting, wanting to read it through without making a mistake, 'If you have a vampire a werewolf or ghost, call Blue Moon and we'll make it toast,' my voice was dripping with false enthusiasm.

Mr Coruthers had a question, 'Are you saying that you don't investigate the paranormal?'

That was the point at which my calm snapped, 'No, I damned well don't,' the outburst surprised me. I prided myself on always remaining calm, so I was more stressed by my venture than I had admitted to myself. This was my first time running my own business, the doubt regarding the decisions I had been making now bubbling to the surface. There had been no trace of nervousness yesterday when I went to bed, but this morning, with the daylight beginning to lighten the world beyond my window, I had felt my confidence slipping, but then I had to concede that over the last few months everything in my life had changed.

Since leaving school I had been employed by Queen Elizabeth herself as a solider in the British Army. Eighteen years had slipped by until, in December of last year, I had taken off my uniform for the last time and shuffled off to be a civilian.

Today, I became a business owner, a path I had chosen for myself, but which was suddenly crushing me flat with worry. Faced with infinite choices, I had been swayed toward working for myself as a private investigator. Finding premises, buying equipment and stationary, setting up a bank account had all been joys to undertake. Even researching where best to advertise and market myself had been fun, but it all led to today and I had no idea if the phone would ever ring.

Of course, the phone ringing was something I worried about before I saw my joke of an advert. Now I was the proud owner of a business that looked to have little chance of success since my advert was going to be considered nonsense by everyone that saw it. It would be seen though. A half page ad stood out, which was why I had ponied up the cash for it.

At the other end, Mr Coruthers asked, 'Can I call you back?'

I answered with a question that I already knew the answer to but felt was worth asking since it would transfer some of my stress to someone else, 'Can you change the advert and reprint your paper?'

'Yes absolutely,' he replied, his voice suddenly bright because he was able to answer a question with a positive response.

'Today?' I enquired, again knowing the answer already.

'Well, err, actually no. It would be in two weeks' time when the next edition is published.'

I pressed home my concern pointlessly, 'What good is that, Mr Coruthers? I am in business now.'

The conversation went back and forth for a few minutes while I posited whether I had a right to sue and he tried his best to placate me though he had no tools with which to do so.

As our discussion reached a natural conclusion, the cell phone in my pocket started to ring. Still talking to the editor, I pulled the phone from its resting place to see who it was. I was expecting to see the name *Mother* displayed on the screen. She would be calling to congratulate me on my first day of business. All I saw was a number though; an unknown caller. I switched it to silent and let it ring out.

Mr Coruthers asked if he could get back to me while he tried to work out how the error had occurred. I let him go but finished by pointing out that the root cause was moot from my position. It would change nothing, so his investigation was purely for his own purposes, not mine.

With the office phone handset back in its cradle, I pushed my chair away from the desk, tilted the back and slouched into it. Renting the office furniture, buying equipment and taking a few courses to learn new skills had all cost money. I was relatively risk-averse when it came to money. It was so hard to come by and so easy to spend that it always felt disrespectful to squander it unwisely. Which is to say that I would never gamble but my investment in the business had been just that: an investment. Seed money in a start-up firm of my own. I had been paid a lump sum as a gratuity for my years of service so I was free of debt and could, in theory, afford for this venture to fail. At least that was what I told myself as I stared at the ceiling. I didn't want it to fail though. I had no other plan for my employment and no desire to start trawling the classified ads looking for a job. The miswritten advert was a problem because I believed a first impression could only be made once. My audience were the people in the local towns and cities, many of whom would see the paper today and assume either that the advert was a joke of some kind, or that the owner was a total kook. Either way, I would get no calls and if I readvertised in two weeks with the text corrected, the chances were people wouldn't even look at it.

I started thinking in terms of recovery plan. How long would it take to create a phoenix firm with a new name? Doing so would mean not only changing the business name though. I would need new business cards and new stationary plus I would have to close down and pay to register a new firm at companies' house and all the tax forms that went with it. I would have to change the sign outside the office and all of that expense would come while billing not one penny until the advert ran correctly in two weeks' time and I could hope the phone might finally ring.

I was calming down as I worked the problem in my head. There would be bills, however, the paper had a responsibility for their error. I would convince Mr Coruthers to assist with the outlay.

My cell phone rang again.

It was the same number as last time. I answered it, 'Blue Moon Investigations, Tempest Michaels speaking.'

'Hello. Is this the firm that deals with the paranormal enquiries?' It was a man's voice, his accent local and the timbre suggesting that he was young. I assessed those elements in the space of a heartbeat, but I didn't know how to answer his question. 'Hello?' he repeated after I failed to reply.

'Yes, sorry. You read the advertisement in the Weald Word?' I was going to have to explain the error how many times?

'I need your help, man!' he wailed, 'My wife has been replaced by a ghoul. I couldn't believe it when I saw your advert this morning. I've got your address, I'm on my way to you now. I'll be there in half an hour,' he disconnected before I could explain the mistake.

The poor chap was going to have a wasted journey, so I made to call him back but before I could swipe the screen and press a button to make the call, the phone leaped into life again with another incoming call.

'Blue Moon Investigation, Tempest Michaels speaking.'

'Ah, Mr Michaels was it?'

'Yes.'

'Jolly good. I am in need of your services, I believe,' the gentleman caller was distinctly less flustered than the last one and more senior in years. Perhaps pensionable age, he spoke well, like a TV announcer, 'My name is Richard Claythorn, you may recognise it.'

He stopped speaking as a cue for me to start, the name meant nothing to me though, 'Sorry, no. How may I help you?'

There was a disappointed noise from the man, a crestfallen sigh as if his name ought to be known by me along with everyone else. 'Mr Michaels, I have a celebrity stalker. I was a film star a few years ago and have attracted the unwanted attention of a man that I believe to be dangerous.'

This sounded more like it. I started making notes on the pad in front of me, 'Please tell me more,' I implored.

'This is not my first stalker, you understand. I enjoyed a long career on the silver screen, picking up my share of admirers and nutters as one does. A few weeks ago, I started seeing the same man outside my house all too regularly. I confronted him one morning, at which point I discovered that he had been writing to me for years. He wanted me to join his pack, you see.' Pack? 'And didn't believe that I was just an actor. He got quite upset when I denied his claims and refused to let him in.' I typed Richard Claythorn into a search bar. 'Now the letters have turned threatening but the police won't do anything because the man hasn't committed a crime and always disappears when I call them.'

The screen filled with images. I groaned internally. Richard Claythorn was an actor, just not a very good one. He had starred in a succession of B movies in the eighties, almost all of which cast him as a werewolf. The first movie had been a success, I had accidentally caught a chunk of it myself at some distant point in the past, but his success had been short lived as he had not been able to escape the role, eventually finding himself typecast as a werewolf in much the same way that Leonard Nimoy could never be seen as anyone other than Spock from Star Trek.

I asked a question, 'How is it that you believe I will be able to help you, Mr Claythorn?'

'The man thinks he is a werewolf. I have to say that he looks like one and for all I know the werewolf legend is true. Just because I was acting doesn't mean supernatural creatures aren't real. I want you to catch the man before he hurts me.'

I was thinking fast now. I had a case. Sort of. Or rather, I had a case that was a load of rubbish but might actually pay the bills. As I was framing my response, I heard the door to my office open. The office sits above a travel agency in Rochester High Street and was accessed by a door at street level around the back. A rickety wooden staircase behind the ground floor door led to another door at the top through which my small office could be accessed. The building was erected in 1804. It said so on a stone plate set into the front façade. Quite what its original purpose might have been, I had yet to find out, but my office had been a store room for the travel agency below until I took occupancy.

A face appeared through the window in the door as the person coming up the stairs neared the top. I thought he must have a couple of stairs left to go, but he was turning the door handle already. When it opened, I saw that he was simply shorter than I had expected.

The man could see I was on the phone, gave a little wave of acknowledgement rather than speak and took a chair when I smiled politely and indicated that he should. I wondered who he was since it could not be the man with the wife for a ghoul I had spoken with just two minutes ago.

9

'Mr Claythorn, I need to conduct some research and come back to you. May I please take an address where I can find you. I already have your number.' I listened as he recited his address and requested that I call him back within the hour to confirm I was taking his case. As I hung up the phone, the man in the chair leaped up to shake my hand. I had no idea who he was but I met him with equal enthusiasm. I had no reason not to. Yet.

'Greetings,' he said, 'Frank Decaux at your service.' Frank was a mousy little man, with a thin frame and a gaunt face. He was roughly five feet five inches tall and weighed perhaps ninety-five pounds.

'Good morning,' I replied. 'I'm...'

'Tempest Michaels,' he answered for me, 'Paranormal detective,' Frank was smiling in an excited manner, 'I cannot tell you how happy I am to have someone fighting the dark forces that threaten our very existence.' I decided to keep my mouth shut. It was already a strange day and getting no better. My visitor wanted to speak, so I would listen and learn. 'Tell me, what was your first supernatural encounter? What brought you into this line of work? Are you imbued with magic abilities?'

I held up my hand to stop him out of fear that the torrent of questions might continue unabated if I did not. He lapsed into careful silence, waiting excitedly for my responses.

'Frank, right?' He nodded. 'Frank... Frank why don't we start with you telling me about your line of work. You already know what my advert says,' I had crafted my reply to tell him nothing and quite specifically avoid answering the questions he had posed.

'Yes, yes, of course. Always wary of otherworld spies disguised as humans. You certainly know your stuff. I'll just prove myself then.'

Now thoroughly curious, I leaned forward to see what he was doing. He had pulled a small packet from a pocket and was unzipping it. A salt shaker came out which he used to pour a small heap of white grains on my floorboards. Then, quick as a flash, he stabbed the end of a finger with a tiny blade that looked to be not only silver but also inscribed with strange runic sigils. He then squeezed a drop of blood into the salt while reciting a quiet chant in a language I neither understood nor recognised. Finally, he settled back into his chair with a wide, satisfied grin, 'See? Quite human. I run an occult bookshop just around the corner. It allows me to stay in touch with practitioners and provide them with knowledge as well as acting as a repository of collected knowledge on the paranormal. I guess you could call me a librarian of sorts. I don't fight, I wish I could, but I recognise where my skills lie and do what I can to support those that do. When I saw your advert this morning, I left my assistant to run things and came directly here.'

'You offer advice and knowledge?'

'Yes.'

'On the paranormal?'

'Yes.'

'For free.'

'Of course. How could I charge for a service that saves lives?'

I considered that for a second. The man might be bonkers, but he might also prove to be useful if I took the Claythorn case on. I had accepted in my head that I might have to. There were bills to pay after all.

'Frank, I have a confession.' I could not only see little need for subterfuge, but also believed that I wasn't clever enough to pretend to be a paranormal investigator for very long so would look stupid soon enough if I tried. 'The advert is a typo.'

His face was etched with questions.

'I am not a paranormal detective. I have never had a paranormal encounter and without wishing to dispute your belief system, I don't believe in anything remotely paranormal. The advert should have said Private Investigator.'

'Oh,' his two-letter answer failed to capture the disappointment on his face, 'so, you don't believe in ghosts?'

'Nope.'

'What about vampires and werewolves?'

'I'm afraid not.'

'How about witches? You must believe in witches.'

'Well, yes, obviously I believe in witches.'

'Really?' he asked suspiciously.

'Of course not, Frank. It's all utter hokum. Demons, wizards, sorcerers, dragons, aliens, Freddie Kruger and the Loch Ness monster are all in the same daft category of entertaining fiction.'

He steepled his hands in front of his face, thinking, 'Wasn't that a client on the phone when I came in?' he asked. I offered him a single eyebrow lift, 'Sorry for eavesdropping,' he added. 'It sounded like a werewolf case.'

'In theory it is. I will prove, however, that it is just a person with an overactive imagination.'

Frank fished in his pocket to produce a business card. It was a little crumpled and worn unlike the shiny brand-spanking new ones I had only taken from their packet yesterday.

'I'm going to leave you my card, Mr Michaels. Just in case you have a question for me at any point. There are so many supernatural creatures invading our plane that I fear you may need me sooner than you expect.'

I took the card and shook his hand as he stood to leave. Frank was mad, but also likeable somehow. The chance of me ever calling his number was slim to none, but I slipped his card into a drawer when he left anyway.

First Client. Thursday, March 18th O94lhrs

THE MAN WITH THE ghoul for a wife turned up at 0941hrs. I was stirring milk into a cup of tea at the time but heard the bottom door open and footsteps hesitating with uncertainty at the foot of the stairs.

I poked my head around the corner. 'Good morning. If you are looking for Tempest Michaels, you are in the right place.'

He blinked, but didn't speak, then put his head down and started up the stairs toward me. He was a man in his mid-thirties, much the same as me in height, weight and age. As he reached the top of the stairs, I saw his face properly for the first time. He had a slight deformation of his nose where it slanted slightly to the left, like a boxer's wound after a fight. His hair was cut short into a long crewcut, maybe half an inch in length and the same length all over as if it had been shaved to his head and all grown at the same rate.

I put my hand out to shake, 'Tempest Michaels.'

'Alan Mayfair,' he replied, giving my hand a good grip in return.

'Would you like a tea? The kettle has just boiled.' I was about to sip mine so failing to offer would just be rude.

He gave it a moment of thought. 'Ah, no. No, thanks. Is it alright if we just get on with it? I am supposed to be at work.'

I indicated a pair of chairs by the window, 'Of course.' I had decorated the room myself a little more than two weeks ago, planning where the desk would go and considering where I would sit to interview clients. The office was a drab little space with one redeeming feature, well two actually if you consider the location right in the middle of the hustle of the town and a few metres from the castle and cathedral. The feature I was referring to though, was the pair of windows that looked out over the High Street. They provided natural light all day long as they faced south and were a perfect location for a small table and two chairs which I found in a second-hand shop twenty yards from the office. The office itself was something I had stumbled across. I had looked at commercial property websites for many hours but failed to find anything that spoke to me. I was trying to be frugal because I couldn't estimate how much income I would attract. Not in the first month, first quarter, first year or ever. There was no benchmark to measure against. There were no private investigators in the area. Not one in the whole phone book, but that was one of the drivers behind setting up the business.

So here I was, talking to my first live client. If only he wasn't stark-raving mad, I might be able to make some money from it.

'Alan, please explain how it is that you believe I can help,' I had a notebook out and a pen poised in my right hand. This would be good practise for when I had genuine clients.

'I need you to dispatch the creature that has replaced my wife.'

I set my pen down. 'When you say dispatch, you mean...'

'Kill it. Burn it. Cut it into little pieces and boil it in holy oil. I don't know how to kill a ghoul, but surely this is what you do for a living?' he was speaking in an animated manner, excited and breathless and desperate. I wanted to laugh at the absurdity of his request. What stopped me though was the realisation that he was serious and the further inevitable conclusion that he might try to do the job himself if I didn't convince him not to.

How do I approach the subject though? I opened my mouth to speak, reconsidered what I was going to say and tried to start again. I must have looked indecisive because I went through that process three times before I worked out how to speak.

'Alan, before any dispatching can take place, it will be necessary to confirm what species we are dealing with. There are so many supernatural creatures invading our plane that I have to catalogue them for the senior council.' I was making it up as I went along, and he was buying every word. 'Can you describe her to me, please?'

'You mean how she looks now?'

'It might be wise to start with how she used to look so you can contrast the changes.'

Once again, I picked up my pen. This time, when he spoke, I started to write. He had been married for nine years. His wife Beatrice had been a cute, petite lady with brunette hair cut in a jaw-length bob. I asked her dress size, but he didn't know, which for me was the mark of an inattentive husband though I kept the thought to myself. Obviously, they had both aged, he said, but he had begun to suspect there was something wrong with her a few months ago when her behaviour became erratic. Her hair had become increasingly long and greasy, her complexion was pallid, her skin glossy and her figure had changed drastically; weight gain visible all over her body, though most notably on her belly.

I had gone along with my charade of taking the case for three reasons: I thought it would be good practise for real clients, I was curious to hear what he has to say and because I didn't know what else to do with him. However, as the meeting progressed, I started to wonder if there might genuinely be something for me to investigate. Mr Mayfair was worried, that much was evident, but I had to ask him what he was worried about.

'My safety,' he replied.

'Do you think your wife is a danger to you now?'

'Have you heard nothing I said? It's not my wife! It's a ghoul of some kind and there's no way I'm returning home until it is gone. I need someone to kill it. If that's not you then I need to stop wasting my time here.' He stared right at me, 'Well?'

Clearly, he expected immediate action. I flipped a mental coin. It landed stupid side up, so I was going to play this out just a little further. 'Mr Mayfair, I think you should leave me your address and a key and go to work. I need to enter your house. Do I have your permission to do that?'

He slumped with relief, 'Yes, yes. Whatever you need. Now, what is this going to cost me?'

The subject of money couldn't be overlooked for long, I was in this caper to make a living, but now I faced a conflict: There was no ghoul and I wasn't going to kill his wife so what should I charge him? I was going to visit his house because I felt I needed to and based on the belief that his wife might actually be ill. The man was a cretin, that much I knew for sure, but was it fair to take his money? I reasoned that since I was already having my time employed and now needed to drive my car and use up even more time, there was no option but to charge him. Additionally, if I opted to do nothing, he might try to rid himself of the ghoul with a handy axe or other tool from his garden shed.

No, I had to investigate and therefore I could feel justified when I handed him a bill.

I had devised standard hourly rates, but I wasn't sure they would apply in what I assumed was a case that required nothing more than a knock on the door. I fished a figure from the air and offered it to him as a day rate charge. He snapped my arm off, signed the paperwork I had and scurried away to work.

Then, as he went out the door, he paused because he had a final, final thought. 'Can you send me a photograph of the body, so I know it is dead?'

Now I was stuck. I wasn't going to kill anyone and was now thoroughly curious about what I was going to find when I arrived at his house. I gave him an evasive answer, 'I will advise you in due course.'

He nodded, tapped the doorframe in thought and was gone.

I was having a bizarre day.

Research.
Thursday, March
18th 1002hrs

MY NEXT TASK WAS to look into Richard Claythorn a little more closely. He was expecting a call back soon, in fact, any second now since my hour was almost up. I liked punctuality and people that met deadlines, therefore I was never late to arrive anywhere and when I said I would call within the hour, I meant it.

I had a few minutes though, time enough to determine if I should take the case or not. Possibly time to work out what the case really was. I wanted to categorise it as a stalker case. That was what he had said, but most stalkers don't come with a werewolf fantasy add on. Did that matter? I pursed my lips as I decided that I didn't know if it mattered, but my ability to pay my bills did.

Between Mr Mayfair and his ghoul and whatever Mr Claythorn's case turned out to be worth, I might even do okay this week and okay was a pleasing step change from an hour ago when I thought I wasn't going to make a penny.

The computer beckoned. What was I researching though? Werewolves? Surely not. I started with Richard Claythorn but soon determined that there wasn't much to learn. He could be classified as a semi-successful actor in that he had enjoyed film roles and a few TV stints and at one point, a thriving fan club. The last bit was most likely because he had been a sexy werewolf and took his shirt off a lot. The career had faltered in the eighties when he was in his late thirties. His last recorded outing as an actor of stage, film, or TV was an episode of The Bill in 1995 when he had played geezer number three in an episode entitled, "You Can't Teach an Old Dog". It was hardly a notable role.

He was single but had been linked with a vast array of eligible ladies in his hey-day. None of them had stuck around long enough to bear children though, so the retired actor was a childless bachelor. I pondered that fate for a second; it was something my mother continually threatened would happen to me if I didn't find a nice lady and settle down soon.

My single status wasn't for lack of trying.

Forcing myself back to the task at hand, I figured that for completeness I would need to examine werewolf legend as well. It was not something I ever thought I would do. I didn't even watch horror films although I will admit I have caught a few of the classics such as Nightmare on Elm Street and An American Werewolf in London. What was the deal in that film? If you survived a werewolf bite, then you became a werewolf at the next full moon?

What rubbish.

A simple internet search returned a deluge of information about werewolves. More than I could imagine had been written including papers by persons with letters after their names. My wide eyes stayed that way as I read a few lines from one such paper entitled: The Origin of the Lycanthrope Legend. Written by an Oxford professor, it was instantly clear that he considered the possibility of supernatural creatures to be real. Furthermore, I had mistakenly believed the werewolf to be a relatively new invention, like Bram Stoker's Dracula or Mary Shelly's Frankenstein, but the werewolf legend went back hundreds of years. I found one reference to a man called Petronious in AD 27.

My slightly-blown mind managed to inform me that I needed to make a phone call, though I kept reading as I hit the button to dial Richard Claythorn's number.

'Richard Claythorn.'

'Mr Claythorn, this is Tempest Michaels of the Blue Moon Investigation Agency. I will be taking your case,' my eyes were still swiping left to right across the screen as I spoke to him.

'Jolly good.'

'I need to come to your house, Mr Claythorn. I have the address. When would be convenient?'

'I'm having lunch with some friends. I should be back around two-ish. Can you come then?'

I changed the time in my head. Two-ish was no kind of time at all. 'I will arrive at 1400hrs.'

'Hmm? Can you come at two or not?' he asked, some impatience in his voice.

I sighed. I was still getting used to civilians and their inability to tell the time correctly, 'Yes, Mr Claythorn. I will see you at... two,' I had to grit my teeth to say the last word.

That gave me almost four hours to play with, but I was a little lost on the subject of what I was supposed to do next. Now that I thought about it, it wouldn't have mattered what cases I had taken today, I would have been filled with the sense of being lost at sea anyway. It was my first day as a private investigator, I had no experience to draw on, nothing in my military service had prepared me for the role and now I had two cases, albeit daft paranormal cases, and no real idea how I was going to solve either of them.

I guess my expectation had been that a logical approach, some hard work and following my instincts would do it. Now I wasn't so sure. Doing nothing was even less likely to get the job done though so I pushed back my chair, slipped my phone into my pocket and went out the door.

I had an address for Alan Mayfair. It was a starting point but before I got to the bottom of the stairs, the door beneath me opened.

'Cooee,' called my mother as she came through the door. I froze in place, mentally calculating whether I could get back up to my office and climb out of the window before she saw me.

I couldn't.

'Oh, hello, Tempest,' she said as she looked up to find me motionless a few feet above her. 'I thought I would come and see how your first day was going and maybe let you treat me to some lunch.'

Lucky me.

'Sorry, mum, I'm just going out, I have a case to investigate.' In my head, I was wondering whether to tell her about the advert. While I thought about that, I asked, 'Where's dad?'

'He's at the chiropodist getting his bunions looked at,' she replied. 'So, where are we going for lunch?'

'I can't go for lunch, mum. For one thing it's not even 1030hrs yet,'

'1030hrs,' she repeated. 'You do know that is not how people talk.'

I ignored her opinion because it was wrong. 'And I just told you I have a case to investigate. I have to go.'

'Oh, that sounds fun. I'll come with you,' my mother replied happily as she turned and went back out the door onto Rochester High Street, 'then we can stop for lunch later.'

Here's a thing about my mother: she is a royal pain in my butt. For years she has been trying to marry me off to any eligible woman that came along. Her desperation for grand-children had manifested at some point in my mid-twenties when her biological grandmother clock started ticking and she had somehow expected me to already be married and filling prams. I had once, at twenty-eight, I think, made the mistake of taking a girlfriend to a family event whereupon my mother had seized the poor girl's attention and grilled her on her intentions, genealogy and menstrual cycle. I never saw her again but my mother took no blame, instead advising me that she clearly wasn't right for me. I was quite ready to settle down if the right woman came along, but actively looking for a wife just sounded crazy. Besides relationship guidance, my mother was very happy to advise me what I was doing wrong on pretty much any subject because she knew best about everything from global politics to global warming, space travel to nuclear physics. Despite all that, she was my mum and she was lovely provided I avoided a long list of controversial subjects. That she thought it was a good idea to come with me on my first case on my first day, came as no surprise.

'Mother, you can't come with me.'

'Why ever not?' she demanded.

'Because... it would be inappropriate. The nature of the case is sensitive,' I said only sort of lying to her.

'What is sensitive about it? Is it to do with a lady? I bet it will help if I am there, you are always terrible with women.' She had already made her way to the passenger door of my car and was waiting for me to plip it open.

I swore silently as I acknowledged that I could let her in and take her with me or I could argue for an hour and then let her in and take her with me. Either way, I was going to have to try to convince her to stay in the car when we arrived.

Mrs Mayfair. Thursday, March 18th 1041hrs

THE ADDRESS WAS JUST outside Ashford in a village called Little Chart. Mother pointed out a charming tearoom on the right-hand side of the road as I came off the motorway. Seeing it caused my tummy to rumble its emptiness. Keeping my eyes on the road, I asked my passenger to pass me the apple I had in my bag by her feet.

'Shall I cut it up for you?' she asked producing a Swiss Army knife from her handbag. 'I keep this handy in case there is ever wine but no bottle opener.'

I couldn't decide if the offer was my mother trying to be helpful or whether she believed I still needed my food cut up for me like I had when I was five. I shook my head and thanked her as I took it from her hand.

'Suit yourself,' she said because she liked to find insult where she could.

The apple was reduced to a skinny core two minutes later when I pulled up outside number forty-three Chidding Street. The house was a cottage in a terraced row of cottages. Each was painted a different colour, but not as a deliberate tactic I thought, more that each had been painted by the owner at some point and each had selected the colour they wanted. The Mayfairs' house was a pastel green, the paint a few years old and flaking in one corner under the eaves.

'These are pretty,' mum said.

I nodded, 'Now you do remember that you promised to stay in the car, yes?' I felt I needed to hammer the idea home. It had taken me most of the journey to convince her that I had to go in alone, eventually winning by explaining that she had done such a great job of raising her son that he needed to stand on his own now.

'Yes, yes, Tempest. Just don't be too long. Your car is too close to the ground. It makes me feel like I am sitting on the road.'

Don't insist on coming with me then.

I left the thought unspoken, patted her hand and went to investigate my first case. A narrow path split the front garden in two even halves. At the end of it, I reached a front door made of wood. There was no doorbell, but perhaps the electronic device would be out of place in this quaint setting. I grasped the iron knocker and used it to rap hard on the door twice.

I stood back a few feet to wait. I had no idea if Mrs Mayfair was home. There were cars in the street, but the houses didn't have drives so they could belong to any one of the homes on the street. Alan had described his wife as a ghoul, he seemed afraid of her but I felt no trepidation as I heard the lock mechanism turning.

I fixed a pleasant smile on my face and prepared myself for the person opening the door to be less than pleasant to look at. As it swung open to reveal the short woman inside, I laughed. It was an involuntary action that burst from my lips before I knew it was coming.

Alan Mayfair had described his wife as ghoulish, that she had been gaining weight for months, and that her hair, which had once been attractive and well-groomed was now lank and lifeless. She was sweaty and bloated, his petite gymnast wife replaced by a creature that shuffled around the house. He wasn't inaccurate in his description, but his diagnosis was wrong. His wife hadn't been replaced by a ghoul. She was just pregnant.

'Good morning. My name is Tempest Michaels. Are you Beatrice Mayfair?'

I got a suspicious look from beneath the slightly greasy mop of hair, 'What's left of her,' she said. 'Are you selling something? Because this really isn't the time.'

'Oh, you're pregnant. How lovely,' said my mother. She was standing right beside me having had no intention of staying in the car.

I kept my eyes focused on Mrs Mayfair when I handed over my card and said, 'Your husband hired me to investigate a case for him. May I come in?'

She squinted at me suspiciously, 'He hired you?'

'Yes.'

'As in, he gave you money to perform a service?'

'Yes.'

'I'm gonna kill him,' her response came through gritted teeth, but she invited me in despite her anger and led me through to her lounge where she had a leather office chair set to its highest position. There were two other women in the room that I took to be her mother and grandmother. They were both sat in armchairs with their legs tucked to one side and a cup of tea held with both hands. They looked up as I followed Mrs Mayfair into the room trailed by my mother.

To answer their curious expressions, Mrs Mayfair said, 'This gentleman is a private investigator. Alan hired him to annoy me.' It was an odd thing to say, but I let it go.

My mother spoke before I could though, 'I'm his mum,' she explained though I doubted the ladies hadn't already realised the relationship.

Mrs Mayfair levered herself into the office chair looking very uncomfortable. 'I have to sit on this or I can't get back up,' she explained. The TV was tuned to a daytime show that I didn't recognise. She grabbed the remote to kill the screen, 'What exactly did my idiot husband employ you to do?'

'He believes you have been replaced by a ghoul,' I delivered the statement with as little inflection as I could manage.

She was looking at the card in her hands, 'Are you a paranormal detective?' she asked.

'No, not at all.'

Her brow furrowed in confusion, 'Why then are you looking into ghouls? That seems like a very specialised thing to investigate.'

'Yes, Tempest, why are you investigating ghouls?' asked my mother. She moved around to stand in front of me so that I now had four women looking at me.

'I needed the work,' I said. It was a lie but only sort of because I really did need the work and it was far easier than trying to explain the advert mix up. Especially where my mother was concerned because she would have a million questions about how it had happened and why didn't they question it and on and on until I made a noose with my belt and hung myself from a light fitting.

'Well, it seems like a very odd case to take if you want to be taken seriously, Tempest,' Mother was steering toward lecture zone.

'Now is not the time, mother,' I assured her.

'It's the perfect time,' she countered, 'these ladies won't mind.' She checked behind herself and backed into the corner of a couch then looked across at the tea service set on a low table hopefully, 'Is there tea in the pot?'

'Err, yes,' said Mrs Mayfair's mum, 'Help yourself.'

Mum got up again and crossed to the table. 'Are there any more cups?' she asked.

'I'll get one, dear,' said Mrs Mayfair's grandmother as she set her own cup down and got up.

I shook my head and prayed to any god that might be listening.

Mother wasn't finished torturing me though, 'Tempest uses a mug for his tea. Can you believe it?'

'Oh, I know,' replied Mrs Mayfair's mother, 'all the kids are doing it now. They serve tea in a coffee mug like heathens.'

'It tastes the same, mother,' complained Mrs Mayfair, rubbing her distended belly and grimacing.

Her mother muttered something that sounded like, 'Youth of today.' But masked her mouth behind her cup as she did.

The grandmother returned with a fresh cup and saucer and a small silver spoon and offered to make it for my mother which precipitated a battle to be the most gracious.

Mrs Mayfair rolled her eyes and looked at me, 'You said my husband hired you to work out if I have turned into a ghoul, yes.'

'Yes.'

'Then what?'

Ah. Now I was on tricky ground. Explaining that I had been asked to dispatch her felt like walking onto a trapdoor. Lying felt like a worse idea though so I opened my mouth and admitted the truth.

All the women in the room took a sharp intake of breath except for my mother, who was instantly on her feet and getting in my face, 'How dare you threaten this poor girl, Tempest? What has gotten into you?'

'Mother will you please calm down, you daft old bat. I'm not here to hurt anyone.' She looked confused. 'Think about it. If I didn't take the case and work out what he was up to, he might have hired someone else or tried to do the job himself.'

'Oh,' she said, 'I hadn't thought of that.'

As my mother picked up her tea again, I looked across at Mrs Mayfair. Her shoulders had slumped and her head was down. She was muttering something I couldn't hear although it sounded suspiciously like she was plotting to cut off appendages he probably wanted to retain. When she looked back up, she said, 'Can you write me a statement to the effect of what you just said?'

I frowned wondering what was happening now, 'May I ask to what purpose?'

She sat back in her chair, her right hand cradling her belly, 'I kicked my husband out two months ago. He was cheating on me because I am too uncomfortable to have sex with him and now that he has been served with a notice of divorce from my solicitor, he has taken to plaguing me with dirty tricks. I'm afraid yours is the latest in a series of stupid pranks designed to make me angry. Stupidly, he doesn't realise that he is just giving me, and my solicitor, more ammunition. So, if you would be so kind, a simple statement explaining that he called you and engaged you to perform this task.'

I really didn't want to end up as a name on a divorce but her husband, my client, had used me. Worse yet, what he had really wanted me to do, was kill her. I had to wonder what he had expected, but perhaps when he read the stupid advert in the paper, he had imagined a Van Helsing wannabe that would dispatch his wife before asking questions. I had to ask myself what Frank might have done. He seemed bonkers enough to want to kill a ghoul.

I nodded, 'I can do that.'

My mother was staring at the pregnant lady now though in a way that made the hair on the back of my neck itch. 'Beatrice is it?' she asked. Beatrice nodded. 'Beatrice, are you saying you are now without a man to help you raise the baby?'

Oh, my word.

'Mother, we are leaving.' My mother flicked her gaze between me and the pregnant lady. 'Now, mother,' I insisted as I turned my own gaze to Mrs Mayfair, 'I will write your report tonight and email it to you.' I noted her email address, thanked her for her patience and wished her luck with the imminent baby.

Mother was muttering as she finished her tea and set the cup and saucer back on the table, 'This is why you are single,

Tempest. You never seize the opportunities you are presented with. I will never get a grandchild at this rate.'

I really wanted to point out that Beatrice's baby wouldn't be mine no matter what course of action I took, but I recognised the futility of any further discussion on the subject. Thankfully, mum's phone rang as we left the house to interrupt her flow. It was dad calling and though I could only hear one half of the conversation, it was clear that mum had abandoned him at the chiropodist and walked to my office leaving him to make his own way home after getting his feet mangled. Now he wanted some lunch and was requesting she returned home because his feet were too sore to do it for himself.

I felt nothing but relief as I drove her home and dropped her off while explaining that I couldn't come in because I had more work to do. As I drove away from her house, shaking my head at the events of the day, my phone began ringing in my bag. The screen in the car displayed a mobile number I didn't recognise, 'Blue Moon Investigations, Tempest Michaels speaking.' The last time I had a phone to answer, other than my own, I had been in the army still and answered always by giving my rank. Muscle memory had been threatening to catch me out each time I opened my mouth but so far I hadn't got it wrong.

'Is this the ghostbusters?' There was giggling at the other end, the voice was young, like a teenage boy perhaps.

'No, this is Tempest Michaels of the Blue Moon Investigation Agency. How may I be of assistance to you?' I was certain I was being punked but kept my tone and temper even.

'I believe I need your help,' the person at the other end replied, his voice now serious.

'How so?'

'Well,' he started, 'I think I saw a ghost.' The line went dead but not before the mirth-filled voice and whoever was with him burst into fits of laughter. I put my phone away and took a breath to centre myself. There was no sense in feeling anger; as a child I had probably played my part in pranks so this was just the universe balancing itself out. It was day one of my business and so far I had pursued one case that was a complete waste of time and had one ahead of me that was questionable at best. I took another breath, forcing calm into my thoughts.

It could be worse and can only get better. I repeated that a few times though I wasn't sure I believed it. My phone rang again. Another unknown mobile number. I couldn't be certain it was the same number as the last call, but it sure looked like it.

I considered a few options to lead with as a response. My good friend Big Ben was less inclined to act like a gentleman and would probably offer to give the young man's mother something to hang her washing on. I wasn't comfortable leading with an insult though so I calmly answered the phone the same as I had before while telling myself I would block the number afterwards.

It wasn't the boy from before though, it was a much older man, his voice betraying his years as it wobbled slightly, 'H-hello? Are you the gentleman that investigates unusual circumstances?' he asked.

I gritted my teeth and swore at the universe, but answered, 'Yes,' anyway. 'Do you have something you wish me to look into?'

'Um, I'm rather worried you might think I'm making it up,' he came across as nervous and very uncertain, but unlike the boy I had spoken with two minutes ago, I doubted this man was playing a prank.

I decided to do my best to make him feel at ease, 'I can assure you, sir, that whatever you have to tell me will be treated with the strictest confidence and I expect what seems unusual to you, will seem quite regular to a person in my line of work.' Yet again I was pretending that I was a paranormal investigator and had been doing the job for years. It didn't make me happy.

'Oh,' he said, sounding brighter, 'good point. Well, I have a shop you see and, well, I keep getting robbed by The Invisible Man.'

Righto.

When I didn't speak for a few seconds because my brain was trying to process what I had just heard, he said, 'Are you still there?'

'Yes, sorry. I was just thinking that this is the third Invisible Man case this year.' I was babbling lies and I had no idea why other than because everything I said had to be a lie because that was what I was living right now. How had I been brought so low?

I took the man's name and address and told him I would be with him in fifteen minutes. He had a small shop in Brachestham, a small village that was little more than a collection of houses and a church. Out beyond Chatham to the North, I had seen it on a map but had never been there. I figured I had just enough time to get there, check out what the old man was seeing and get home for lunch and dogs before I would need to head off for my 1400hrs appointment with Richard Claythorn.

As I drove, I began to wonder how many calls I would have received if my advert had gone out as planned.

The Invisible Man. Thursday, March 18th 1122hrs

ROCK GROUP QUEEN'S I'M the Invisible Man snuck its way into my head and played itself over and over on continuous loop uninvited as I wound my sleek red sports car through the country lanes to get to the address in Brachestham. I only knew a handful of the words but they persisted anyway so I was glad when I parked in front of Martelle's Grocer Shoppe and I could distract myself.

An old but cheery-sounding bell jingled above my head as I stepped into the shop. Like so many little shops serving a local community, it was packed floor to ceiling with anything and everything that a person could possibly wish to buy. Doubtless all the goods were overpriced in comparison to a supermarket but they would also be priced fairly so the owner could manage to make a living and stay in business. I doubted many small shop owners had yachts for the weekend.

'Hello?' I called out as I made my way through breakfast cereals, toilet rolls and lemonade.

A floor board creaked ahead of me as an elderly gentleman with an apron, wire-rimmed glasses and what appeared to be house slippers stepped out from his counter to see what his customer wanted.

'Good morning. What can I help you with?' he asked politely.

I produced a business card from my pocket, saying, 'Tempest Michaels,' as I handed it over. 'You called me about a theft problem you seem to be suffering.'

The man was staring at the card which he was holding with both hands. 'It doesn't mention that you are a paranormal detective on here,' he pointed out.

'No, it doesn't,' I agreed and left it at that. 'You want me to catch an invisible man, yes?' He nodded, 'What can you tell me about the circumstances that led you to believe you have an invisible burglar?'

The elderly gentleman was called Cyril Martelle. He had been running the shop since he bought it with his wife fifty-three years ago. I refrained from asking where his wife was today as I worried I knew the answer from the sad acceptance in his voice when he spoke about her, but he told me anyway that she had passed eighteen months ago. He didn't elaborate and I made no enquiry. Following her death, he had taken on a shop assistant, a young man, to help him in the shop. Then, twelve weeks ago he had offered his granddaughter a part time job. She was nearly sixteen and his son had expressed that she needed some responsibility because she had fallen in with *the wrong crowd*. Cyril worked in the shop in the day with his assistant and she covered the evenings from 1800hrs until closing time at 2100hrs and most of the day Saturday. They didn't open on a Sunday because that was the sabbath.

The first few times he noticed things missing he hadn't said anything. Then, when it persisted, he asked his granddaughter if she knew where the missing stock was. Nothing like this had ever happened before she started working there so, naturally, he suspected her. He didn't want it to be true and hoped his question would cause her to realise he was on to her and that would be sufficient to make it stop.

It didn't stop though and when he told his son, he had exploded and flat out accused the girl of theft. There was a huge fight, but Cyril apologised because he had no evidence and said his son had over-reacted. She carried on working at the shop and the thefts stopped for a while, then started again. This was about three weeks ago. He lied to his son when he asked if there had been any further instances of missing goods and had a camera installed to watch the shop. The thefts had instantly stopped. However, they restarted again a week later.

Cyril said that watching the recordings was quite boring, even on fast forward but the problem was that he had lots and lots of footage of an empty shop at night with no one in it and his goods were going missing from the shelves during the night without anyone coming in or going out.

'Can you show me?' I asked.

He led me to a back room just behind the counter where an ancient-looking, made from iron not plastic, push-button till sat. 'I don't know how they are doing it Mr Michaels. They don't even ring the bell and I sleep right above it so I would hear it every time.'

I didn't respond. Not yet. I wanted to see the video footage first. There was a small screen TV, not a slim, flat screen one but what we have all now come to think of as giant and chunky. It sat on an old desk in a room that was clearly used for doing the books and ordering stock. Next to it were faded ledgers with labels turned grimy from years of use.

On a shelf above the TV was a box of electronic gadgetry with cables that ran to the TV and through a conduit in the wall into the shop. He explained that it could record a week at a time and helped to keep his insurance costs down. Not that saving money on his insurance was any help because he was losing stock almost every day.

'What sort of stock?' I asked as he set the machine to start playing the footage from the previous night.

'Oh, ah, I have a list if it helps.'

'Yes, please.' Cyril handed me a clip board. Like everything else it was worn with age, the once sharp corners were now rounded from erosion but I liked his apparent policy of buying a thing once and using it to its death. A4 sheets of paper with neat copperplate handwriting listed the goods that had disappeared. A new sheet for each day that he had recorded a loss.

There were a lot of sheets.

A trend was easy to spot though. Chocolate bars, particularly Cadbury Dairymilk, alcohol in the form of wine and sometimes vodka, various tins and packets of food and there were several entries where tampons and condoms had been taken by the invisible thief. As I leafed back through the sheets, making a mental tally in my head I noted that the occurrences grew less frequent as I went back in time. Or, looked at differently, they were getting more frequent now as if the thief were getting more confident.

'Tell me more about your granddaughter please?' I requested while I watched the footage. I had started from its earliest point and discovered it was very simple to control so I could watch until I saw Cyril shuffle through the shop to open up each morning, then leap forward fourteen hours until either he, the granddaughter, or the assistant closed up again.

Cyril had called the assistant a young man, which had caused me to form a mental picture of a chap in his early twenties. He wasn't. The assistant he had hired was a dumpy-looking chap with untidy hair and glasses who must have been fifty or not far from it. His name was Adrian Hemp, he lived in the village in the house his mum left to him and he had never been married. Cyril also told me about his granddaughter. The *wrong crowd* turned out to be a couple of older kids that would hang out in the park and smoke cigarettes. One of them even had a tattoo. To me they just sounded like teenagers, but

I conceded that I would want better for my daughter if I had one.

Watching the CCTV footage, I noticed something. I had to take the film back several times to check what I had seen. 'Have the police watched this footage?' I asked.

'The police? Goodness, no. I couldn't call the police to deal with this. What if they arrested my granddaughter?' I suppose it might make Christmas with the family a little uncomfortable. 'Besides, how do I tell them I have an invisible thief?'

Clearly that had been the thought process that had led him to me. I flicked through the sheets again, noting how often the thefts had taken place recently and reached a decision. I rose from the chair saying, 'I need to check on something.'

In the shop, I examined the bell, looked inside it and ran a wet finger around before touching it back to the tip of my tongue. Then I looked at the cables coming through the wall and where they went to. 'Is there a remote?' I asked.

'A remote?' echoed Cyril.

'Yes, you know, a device to operate the system without pressing the buttons on the machine,' I explained.

He realised what I meant but said that he didn't remember there ever being one. I had a good idea how our invisible man was committing the crime without detection but would have to prove it and catch the person in the act in order to give Cyril the closure he wanted. I checked the rest of the night time video footage, making notes as I saw a pattern develop.

'Cyril, I need to return later this evening. I intend to catch your thief in the act tonight. First though, we need to discuss my fee.' I outlined what I needed to charge, although I will admit now that I am a terrible business man and gave him a reduced rate because I just wasn't comfortable taking his money. I also described what I planned to do but when he asked me how his granddaughter was doing it, I said that I would have to show him.

We shook hands as I left the shop. I was coming back tonight at 2200hrs to lay in wait for Cyril's thief. Right now, though, I was getting hungry and the dogs needed some exercise. Thankfully my house wasn't far away.

Lunch. Thursday, 18th March 1217hrs

WHEN I SET OFF this morning, I had no idea what to expect from the day but had figured that I would have the time to go home for my lunch so I could walk the dogs and deal with their needs. One of the joys of being self-employed was the ability to determine one's own schedule and that was what I was doing.

The house in Finchampstead was a place I had bought a couple of years ago. The housing market had been depressed and at the time, I had recently returned from back to back tours in Iraq which essentially meant I hadn't spent any money in more than a year and had amassed a decent lump sum. The house was in the corner of a cul-de-sac and had a nice garden that wrapped around the house at the back.

I parked on the driveway in front of the house, thinking once again that I needed to get around to planting some shrubs and flowers. The front of the house was tidy and in good condition but a little drab. Some greenery, perhaps a wisteria climbing the side of the house, would break up the harsh edges and provide colour.

A snuffling noise came from the other side of the door as I put my key in the lock, then the sound of claws skittering across the stone tile as I pushed the door open to force the dogs out of the way.

I greeted the two small canines as they buzzed around my feet excitedly. They followed me to the kitchen where I put down my bag and took a knee to fuss them. Bull immediately inverted himself to expose his belly, a tactic designed to make me scratch it. I obliged, the comfort of a dog's affection not to be underestimated.

I shooed them both into the garden where they immediately saw a neighbour's cat lurking near the far wall and shot off barking to repel it. Then, while they snuffled about and found a spot to do their business, I made tea and pulled ingredients for lunch from my fridge. I try to eat healthy as often as I can which is made easier by buying only healthy foods and planning ahead. I had a Tupperware box of quinoa, rice, beans and lentils ready to go, avocado pears in the fruit bowl next to the bananas because they ripened better like that and some chicken thighs marinating in a spice blend. The chicken was dumped into a wok while the rice blend got sixty seconds in a microwave.

The dogs barked to be let in as I was serving my food, the smell of it very distracting to their permanently empty bellies.

Satisfied with some carrot I had sliced them, they left me alone to eat as they crunched their way through it, but still wanted to clean my bowl when they heard my fork scrape the bottom.

Friends and relatives had both questioned my choice of miniature Dachshund as a pet. I like them though. They are cute and funny and because I had two, they looked after each other. The elder one came to me just shy of two years ago, his younger brother just less than a year after that. They were both still very young dogs and Dachshunds are known for being long lived, many making it into their third decade.

With lunch done and the dishes in the dishwasher, I walked them around the village, killing more time before my appointment with Mr Claythorn at 1400hrs. My route took me out of the village through a vineyard to the east. Finchampstead was a small place, I didn't know how many houses there were or what the population was, but my estimates would be maybe five hundred and perhaps two thousand. A road bisected the village neatly down the middle and was the only way in or out unless one went by foot across the fields or through the vineyards that completely surrounded the built area.

After looping to the north and coming back into the village from the west, I had to admit I was running out of tasks with which to kill time. Maybe I didn't need to kill any more of it though. Perhaps I could act like a detective and scope out the area around Mr Claythorn's residence; familiarise myself with the surroundings. If he had a stalker, maybe he was there now, watching the property.

Now I was thinking.

As I settled the dogs on the sofa once more, I reassured myself that I would soon have multiple cases to investigate, real ones, not this daft paranormal stuff, and would laugh about my first day, when I was so green and worried about what I should be doing. With my confidence returning now that I had found something proactive to do, I locked my house and headed to Chatham.

If you are not familiar with Chatham, then it should be explanation enough to say that most people don't slow down if they have to pass through it. It's a bit rough. But saying it is a bit rough is like saying Bruce Lee knew some martial arts. I wouldn't go there at night and I was a soldier for eighteen years.

Mr Claythorn lived on the very outskirts, in a postcode that was closer to the smaller, quieter village of Walderslade than Chatham, so he was away from the nastier side of the town though I wondered what his neighbourhood would be like. One of the disadvantages of my army career was that I spent almost no time in England. I was always somewhere else, so I was unfamiliar with the Nation, even with places close to where I lived.

This was a chance to see what Walderslade was like.

Mr Claythorn's House. Thursday, 18th March 1322hrs

I PARKED AROUND THE corner from the address I had for Mr Claythorn. His place backed into woodland and its position high up on the western slope of Bluebell Hill gave it a commanding view looking down over the Medway Towns. It wasn't a view I considered worth paying for, but it was a view and the house was worth a good deal more than mine.

I looked around for a few minutes. Was there a stalker lurking in the undergrowth? If there was, he was staying concealed. Sitting in my car, I asked myself what the clever move would be if I wanted to catch this person. If he truly was deluded enough to believe in all the werewolf guff then would he be here during the day? Probably not, right? Then I would need to come back at night when he was likely to be around.

Extending my premise though, meant that right now I could move freely and look for signs of an observation post.

I slid from the car, closing the door quietly so the noise would not draw attention, but not so stealthily that I appeared furtive. I doubted the stalker was here, but if he was, I didn't want him to think there was anything out of place in my movements.

I walked by Richard's house while pretending to talk on my phone so I could surreptitiously look about for anywhere that appeared to have a good line of sight to his property. At the corner of the property, I found my way around to the back by climbing over a low fence and heading into the woodland. If someone was watching the house, they weren't necessarily doing it from the front.

A sturdy and relatively new looking fence had been erected all the way around the property. It was over six feet high with a concrete lintel base. Easy to scale but quite hard to look through. However, as I pushed my way through the undergrowth that was just beginning to come back to life after the hard winter, I found a hinged panel. It was at eye height and the ground beneath it was scuffed as if someone had been standing there for long periods. The panel was roughly ten inches wide by six inches high with a hinge at the top. I lifted it to peer through. It provided an unbroken view of the rear of the house, from which I could see inside his living space. If Richard Claythorn was sitting on his couch watching TV or entertaining, I could watch from this position. If he was in his outdoor pool or in his kitchen, I could watch. The whole downstairs rear elevation was glass panelling.

I pushed on but found my way back to the street without finding another spot like it. I wanted to check across the road, where an old public phone box, abandoned, vandalised, and rusting backed into another spot of woodland. There were other houses here, but each was completely detached and snuggled into its own piece of the wood line. A single road ran in, looped around and ran out again.

I shot my cuff to check my watch: 1357hrs. At Mr Claythorn's gate I pushed the buzzer. Nothing happened for a few seconds, then I heard the click of a magnetic lock and a pedestrian gate to the side of the vehicle gate swung open slightly. I pushed through it and entered a well-tended and luscious garden. Even coming out of winter, his lawn was immaculate, and the bushes clipped. A path led along the side of a driveway that curved around to meet the front of the house.

The door opened as I got to it, a man I recognised as Richard Claythorn appeared from within, 'Tempest Michaels?'

'Indeed.' I produced a card from my pocket in a slick move I had shamefully practised in front of a mirror at home. We shook hands and he invited me inside which I discovered was just as plush as the outside. Lots of white marble and elegant oil paintings were in the lobby area the door opened on to and it led to a larger central hub from which a wide spiral staircase ascended, and rooms spoked off in different directions. In the centre, on a plinth was a bronze statue of Richard Claythorn in werewolf form howling at an imagined moon and on the walls were posters of his films. It was a shrine to himself. I considered that I might do the same thing if it were me, but I would have them less prominently displayed.

'Right through here, Mr Michaels, please. Would you like a coffee?' He led me into a large kitchen where he offered me a chair at a table set in the centre of the room. The smell of fresh, strong coffee lingered in the house. I had detected it the moment I came inside, but it was a faint smell, as if from breakfast and couldn't be fresh as I knew he had been out. He had been in long enough to set his machine to make some though. I could see it percolating in one corner of the kitchen counter and it looked about done.

'Coffee would be lovely, thank you.' I pulled a notepad and pen from my bag. 'Mr Claythorn, you said you have correspondence from the man you believe to be stalking you, is that correct?'

He was pouring two mugs of steaming dark brown liquid, his eyes on the task but he answered over his shoulder, 'Yes, emails. Shall I forward them to you?'

'Yes, please,' I could read them later, 'Can you tell me his name, please?'

'No.' He turned and brought the mugs to the table, then fished milk from the fridge and sugar in a bowl with a spoon from the counter. 'What I mean is, he doesn't put his name on his emails. Just an initial: J.'

Very enigmatic and not very helpful.

'I need to ask why it is that you think he might do you harm?' I lifted the mug of coffee to my face and closed my eyes as I let the scent seep into my nose. Then I took an experimental sip. Richard Claythorn spent some money on his coffee, that much was instantly obvious.

Across the table, Richard scratched his head. 'The way he looks at me. It is hatred in his eyes. He looks homeless, which is to say he doesn't look like he has had a haircut in years, and he smells awful. That could just be how he lives of course, but read the emails, please, they explain everything.' He took a sip of his drink. 'I have seen him too many times recently and almost always at night. When I confronted him a week ago, he said the full moon was coming and when it did, he was going to get even.'

'Even for what?' I asked.

Richard just shrugged. 'I don't know. I even asked him, but that made him angrier as if it was something I should know about.'

I continued asking questions as I thought of them, thankful that a torrent of ideas arrived to fill my blank head and make me look like a seasoned professional. Unfortunately, the answer he supplied to almost all of them was a blank. I asked if he had been able to take a picture of the man at any point, but he said it hadn't occurred to him to do so. I asked if the man had any distinctive features that might help me to recognise him, but the answer once again was that he couldn't think of any other than he was scruffy and smelly. I didn't think that was a lot to go on.

The man had first appeared a few weeks ago. He simply rang the bell at the gate much as I had earlier, but Richard had seen the man from the camera attached to the security system and denied him entry. Through the intercom he had asked what business the caller had but the exchange that followed was all to do with Richard being a werewolf and the man wanting him to join his pack. Richard told me he had tried to patiently explain that he was just a movie star and the werewolf the man had seen was nothing more than makeup. It hadn't deterred him though and he was back the next day and the day after that.

Richard called the police, who were good enough to perform a drive by. The man was gone by the time they arrived though and this happened the next time he called them a few days later and yet again just yesterday which had driven him to look for someone that could deal with him. He had found my advert by accident and had called it immediately.

'He seems to know when I am here,' Richard said at one point. 'I have only been home a few minutes some nights when he suddenly appears.'

I thought about the peeping hole in the back fence but didn't mention it. I wanted Richard's behaviour to be as natural as possible until I caught the man and suspected he would constantly stare at the fence if he knew someone might be out there. The loose plan in my head was to set my own observation post and catch the man there later today. Of course, in that plan I was hoping he came here every day, which he might not, but I shrugged mentally at that concern as I was still able to bill the hours to my client if I drew a blank.

Together we killed nearly an hour talking about the case before I exhausted my list of questions and shut my notebook. 'I think I have enough to go on,' I said as I stood up. We had been through my costs and I had him sign a contract, so I was ready to go. I still had no idea who his werewolf was or what he wanted but I had a case. A real case. I was telling myself the werewolf thing was just a distraction and what I was actually doing was investigating a stalking for a high-end minor celebrity client. It certainly sounded better when I framed it that way.

On my way to the door I thought of something. 'Do you happen to know when the full moon is?'

He shot me a wry look as he said, 'Tomorrow.'

Thoughtfully, I nodded. I was going to be back here tonight. We shook hands as he wished me luck and then the meeting was done and it was all down to me.

Batman. Thursday, March 18th 1637hrs

DRIVING AWAY FROM RICHARD'S house, I found myself doing some mental calculation. I was double booked tonight in a way as I had a stakeout to perform in two different locations: Richard's place and Cyril's. My gut was telling me I could begin to watch Richard's house as soon as it got dark and that the man would appear early on, or at least well before midnight if he was going to appear at all. In contrast, the invisible man at Cyril's shop wouldn't show himself until after midnight so I was going back two hours before that to make sure I was ready.

It was a loose plan alright, but I felt it was safe enough to stake out Richard's place for a couple of hours before I headed back to Cyril's. What I had to do first was go shopping. It occurred to me while I was talking to Richard that I didn't have anything to wear for hanging out in bushes in the dark.

When I left the army, I handed all the gear back. I still had a few items that were surplus or that I had bought myself, but other than a pair of black boots, I didn't think I had anything that I could use. There was a shop in Rochester High Street that sold fishing and camping equipment and with it all sorts of knives and other equipment that anywhere else would just look like an array of weapons. Of course, it really was just an array of weapons and that attracted some clients who were not interested so much in camping but more inclined to home defence, and thus the shop held some other items that catered to that person's needs.

Fifteen minutes after leaving Richard's, I was walking through the door of the shop, the innocent little bell that jingled above my head sounding incongruous given the wall of knives I faced inside.

'Help you?' asked a man that I took to be the proprietor. He was standing behind the counter looking a little bored but wearing a professionally interested smile now that he had a potential customer.

'Military surplus?' I enquired.

He pointed across the shop. 'Way over in the back.'

The original purpose of the shop might have been a bakery or a butcher's or anything, but I doubted it had started life two hundred years ago as a camping and outdoor pursuits shop. The age of the place meant the ceiling was lower than one would find in a modern building and gave it a higgledy layout. I found what I was looking for though, which was hardwearing trousers and a top that wouldn't catch and rip if I ran through undergrowth and thorns. Military gear was designed for just that, but I didn't want the traditional hues of green and brown I had worn most of my life. There was plenty of it on the rack, yet I selected black.

Like Batman, one might say, I clothed myself head to toe in black, adding a Kevlar vest with armoured plates in the front and back for stopping bullets and a pair of fingerless gloves that had Kevlar pads on the knuckles. I tried it all on for size, grimaced slightly at the price but conceded that I needed it and would very possibly get to use it many times in the future.

I paid for my goods, took the bags containing my neatly folded clothing and very bulky armoured vest and went back to my car.

The Werewolf. Thursday, March 18th 1917hrs

STAKING OUT RICHARD CLAYTHORN'S house by myself was going to be boring. I knew this because at different points in my army career I had endured mundane duties. That's just how it goes sometimes and quite often they were a welcome change from being shot at. Setting an ambush though is perhaps the worst. As one might imagine, it is impossible to know when the target may arrive or even if they will, and silence is necessary to maintain the element of surprise.

So, as I crept silently and slowly through the dark trees behind Richard's house, light coming from the almost full moon high above, I was ready for a boring couple of hours.

I wasn't disappointed.

Time moves slower when there is nothing happening. In the dark, left alone with just one's thoughts for company, the minutes stretch out to make an hour feel like an eternity. It had been difficult to navigate but I had found my way to a position close enough to the peeping hole that I would see anyone if they were there. It was bathed in moonlight and quite devoid of werewolf/stalker when I arrived. I might have missed him but I was confident I had got into place early enough that he was yet to arrive, if indeed he was coming. It was quiet, although some TV noise and the low hum from the motorway less than half a mile distant were both audible. Certainly, it was quiet enough that no one would be able to approach without me hearing them long before I saw them.

A short few minutes after arriving I had felt my pulse rise as something came through the bushes near the fence. It was just a neighbour's cat though or perhaps a fox.

The worst part of waiting quietly like this is that you cannot look at your watch. Even the ones with a dull glow will illuminate too brightly and give away your position and the watches with the luminous hands are impossible to see. I had noted the moon's position using a prominent tree as a reference when I stopped moving and had been judging time from its movement ever since. I figured I could hang on maybe another thirty minutes or so, assuming my ability to tell the time by the moon was accurate, after which I would have to leave to get to Cyril's place.

Another slow fifteen minutes or so slipped by. The cool March air was beginning to penetrate my clothing and my feet were going numb. The dominant feeling though was boredom. Watching nothing, doing nothing and staying quiet is boring.

Stuff it.

I was leaving. There was no good reason to believe the target known as J would show up tonight or even ever again and I doubted the client wanted to pay for me to hang around all night. It would be cheaper to hire a bodyguard. As I turned to go though, a dark shadow moved through a small patch of moonlight near the corner of the fence. The unmistakable figure of a man had just rounded the corner and was heading my way.

I kept quiet for a second to watch, but a little voice in my head accused me of stalling. I had read about my rights and limitations and discussed them with my tutor on the short residential course I had taken to set myself up as a private investigator. Provided I could show minimal force had been used and I had a defendable reason to believe the person I tackled was engaged in a criminal activity of some kind, I was safe to arrest anyone I saw fit. Now that I was faced with the task though, my pulse was thumping hard enough for the man to hear.

The piece of fence with the peeping hole had a broad swathe of moonlight illuminating it, so when the man stepped into it, I got a much better look at him. There were two things I noticed instantly: He was naked from the waist up and he was hairy as anything. My first thought was that I had already solved the case. The moment he looked through the peep hole I could legitimately restrain him and call the police to whom I would report him for stalking and trespass, and I would have successfully captured the man my client had tasked me with finding and all within a few hours. The sound of a cork popping from a bottle went off in my head.

I took a step forward tentatively. I wanted to close the distance to him before I issued a warning so I could limit the likelihood of him bolting. As I moved though, my plan of attack forming, the man hunched over and began groaning. An arm shot out at an unnatural angle and he contorted his back as he twisted around on the spot. Then the other arm stretched back and I caught the sight of long fingernails that looked more like talons. As the man let out another guttural cry, I realised what he was doing.

He was transforming into a werewolf.

For the first time, I wondered about my safety. I was taller, heavier and more muscular than the man in front of me, but he might be genuinely mental and that was a concern. Genuinely mental people are not only unpredictable but may be more inclined to harm another person as the natural barrier that prevents each of us from doing so is set at a different level.

He crouched down, disappearing into the undergrowth and for a moment I thought he was going to start moving about on all fours. Instead, he stood back up and faced me, the moon showing me glowing eyes and a mouth full of teeth that were anything but human.

Terror gripped me but it lasted no more than a heartbeat as anger stepped up and squashed it back down again. I wasn't going to be afraid of the man in front of me. Not a damned chance.

He tilted his head back and howled, the noise an unearthly wail that started dogs barking in the distance. Then he resumed his slightly crouched pose with his arms to his sides and though he was looking right at me, I realised he couldn't see me; I was in shadow and my face was blackened to remove the shine.

It was game time.

'Good evening,' I said with volume and confidence. The creature damned near jumped out of its skin, but it didn't cuss or even speak, the man able to stay in character despite the scare. I continued, 'My name is Tempest Michaels. I have been employed by the man you are stalking. We need to speak with the police now. I will not harm you in any way, but if you resist or I believe you may harm me I am quite capable of subduing you.'

I had no further need for stealth so while speaking I had stepped out of the shadows and begun crossing the short distance between us. He stood frozen for two seconds, but when I stopped speaking, he started running.

And he was fast.

I couldn't see what he had on his feet but he was shifting gears and leaping over bushes like the route was ingrained in his head. He had twenty feet on me before he got to the corner of the fence and at least thirty before he made the road and could accelerate. I lost him from sight until I got to the road myself, suddenly emerging into the light coming from streetlamps above me. A car was sweeping up the road in my direction, its headlights undoubtedly picking me up as

I sprinted across the road in front of it. I could see my quarry still. He had crossed the road, followed the pavement for a short distance as it went in front of another grand property and had then cut across a wide expanse of grass. As I hit the grass myself, I could see that I was going to lose him in the trees when he reached the far side of the field. There was shouting coming from behind me, the motorist I had ran in front of no doubt. I ignored it as I ran on, my arms pumping to propel me but I was never much of a sprinter.

The blow from behind caught me by surprise.

Tackled around the hips, my feet stumbled as my centre of gravity escaped my control and I pitched forward to land heavily on my face and chest.

A man's voice shouted, 'Stay down,' but the opportunity to resist was quickly snatched away as I felt the cold steel of a handcuff snap around my left wrist to the accompanying sound of a ratchet tooth sliding home. Turning my head, I could see a police uniform. His hat was gone, it was in the streetlight a few yards behind him and just beyond that was a female officer standing next to the squad car, its strobe lights doing a great job of drawing people to the scene.

I was being arrested.

Frustrated, I yelled, 'Nice one, Sherlock. You just tackled the wrong guy. The bad guy is getting away.' He paid no attention to what I was saying though as he recited his practised statement advising me that I was under arrest. Knowing there was nothing to be gained by speaking at this juncture, I sucked in lungfuls of air and offered mute compliance as he helped me off the ground. 'To the car then?' I asked as he wheeled me around and pointed me in that direction, one hand around my right bicep to control me.

His partner was using the radio to tell dispatch they had a person in custody. I wasn't going into the car though, I was quite determined about that. I nodded to the lady in uniform, saying, 'Good evening,' as we drew close. 'You know you tackled the wrong chap. I was chasing the person you should be arresting.'

'Of course, love,' she replied with a fake laugh. 'No doubt you were out walking your dog in the SWAT gear. You're not a burglar at all.' She levered herself off the wing of the car to open the back door so I could be pushed inside.

I kicked it shut. She didn't like that. 'I am a private investigator. My card is in my pocket along with the keys to the shiny red Porsche over there,' I nodded with my head so she could track where I was looking. 'Hardly the car for loading stolen goods into.'

'So, you were here for something else. You are dressed like a terrorist and ran from a police car. You're going to the station.' She opened the door again but I was quite able to make myself immoveable.

Exasperated, I said, 'Seriously? You didn't see the man I was chasing? No shirt on? Looked like a werewolf? None of that ringing any bells?' The two cops stared at me impassively.

It was the female officer that spoke, her notebook now in her hand as she recorded what I had said, 'A werewolf, you say?'

I could see where this was going. 'Look,' I tried, 'I can resist and be problematic and draw this out, or you can knock on one door and ask the resident if he employed me to catch his stalker. A stalker that just happens to believe he is a werewolf.' I was keeping my voice calm and reasonable and offering no threat, but I could see they had no interest in what I was trying to tell them.

I had hoped that telling them how it was I came to be chasing a werewolf at night might help. It had the opposite effect though, as, with a grunt, the male cop went back to his attempt to shove me in the car. 'You don't want to add resisting arrest to the list, do you?' he asked.

'Surely, I am already under arrest, dummy. I am resisting going to the station because I am the innocent party.' On calling the man a name, the lady cop's eyebrows had risen in surprise. She was paying attention though. I aimed an imploring expression at her as I said, 'Please knock on my client's door. He will clear this up.' She looked ready to cave. 'I will even sit in the car while you do it.' The final offer did the trick. I guess maybe the opportunity to avoid processing me and all the paperwork that went with it was attractive, especially if I was in fact innocent.

The lady cop looked about. 'Which door.'

'That one over there,' I said, once again using my head to point. 'The owner is Richard Claythorn. Please tell him you stopped his detective from catching his stalker. I'm sure he will be most pleased since he gave up asking the police for help.'

I probably wasn't helping my cause by annoying them, but I was in the mood to do so.

Somewhat reluctantly, I did as I had promised I would and slid into the back seat of the car. The lady police officer had to press the buzzer a few times in her bid to get an answer. Sadly, despite the lights being on inside, no answer came and as she walked back to the car, the male officer shut the door on me with a resounding thunk.

Chatham Police Station. Thursday, March 18th 2117hrs

I HAD NEVER BEEN arrested before. Never been in trouble with the police and I was trying to find some positives from the experience. I was having to look really hard.

As the lady cop, whose name I had learned was Debbie McHardy, led me in through the back door of the station, a desk sergeant greeted the pair of officers. 'Is this your terrorist slash burglar?' he asked.

Debbie unclipped her radio and took off her hat, placing both on the desk and stretching her neck to loosen it. She said, 'He claims to be a private investigator.' She pulled her notebook from a pocket and read her notes, 'He was in Cox Road because he was employed by a client...' She paused to read further. 'A Mr Richard Claythorn to catch a werewolf that has been stalking him.'

Perfect. That made me sound like an utter nutter.

The desk sergeant offered me a bored expression, 'Get many werewolves in Walderslade?'

Equally bored, I replied, 'It wasn't a werewolf. Just a man that is pretending to be one. My client is an actor that starred in several films in the eighties. Bite of the Werewolf, The Werewolf's Wife.'

'Oh, I know that one,' chipped in Debbie helpfully.

'Yeah. I'm not making it up. I was hired because he couldn't get the police to do anything.' I saw their expressions and knew I had said the wrong thing.

The desk sergeant leaned forward to get in my face. 'Thank goodness for you then. I guess we'll just process you. Check your story out and decide whether we need to charge you or not.'

The police took their sweet time with me. I couldn't say that I blamed them as my arrogant attitude had provoked an unhelpful attitude in return. They popped me in a corner, the handcuffs still on while they worked out what to do with me. It gave me time to rerun things in my head and make a mental promise to remember this point in time when I was next faced with the police. I had to question whether my new career would often put me in contact with them, but instantly provided my own answer that it had to. I had the ability to investigate and find evidence against an individual, but I had no way of bringing criminal charges, of prosecuting or incarcerating persons if they were guilty of something. If the werewolf I had chased tonight later harmed Richard Claythorn all I could do was hand him over to the police for them to deal with.

I was allowed a phone call once I had been messed about for an hour, by which time I was already expected to be at Cyril's shop. It was Cyril that I called. He answered the phone and listened patiently to my explanation. I think it took him by surprise, but he accepted it and agreed to stay up late until I arrived.

'Will this take long?' I had asked at one point.

It was Debbie that looked up, 'As long as it takes, I'm afraid.' Her answer wasn't evasive, and her demeanour had calmed so she was just giving me an honest answer. Despite my appearance, no crime had been reported and through a quick internet search she had proved that I was who I said I was. Their presence in Walderslade had been nothing more than a routine drive by. Bad luck on my part that I ran in front of their car at the exact moment I had.

Even though they elected to release me without charge, I still lost almost two hours and had to grab a cab to get back to Walderslade to collect my car. So, now, three hours later, I was sitting in the dark in the back room of Cyril's shop, and I was being silent and still for the second boring stakeout of the day. Technically, it was the next day, but since I hadn't been to bed yet, I was counting it as my first day of business still running.

Cyril's Invisible Man. Friday, March 19th 0213hrs

EARLIER, WHILE WATCHING THE night time footage on fast forward, I had noticed a blip. A clock in the bottom left corner of the screen displayed the time but it had jumped from 0113hrs to 0116hrs on Tuesday morning this week. Then on Wednesday it had done the same thing at 0037hrs, stopping for a total of two minutes forty-eight seconds. This afternoon I had checked and double checked what I was watching and gone back and forward through the days to see how often it happened, which was six nights out of the last seven.

Someone was switching the CCTV feed off for just long enough to get in and out. They were taking a bag of potato chips, a can of coke, a packet of tampons or whatever they fancied that night. All small quantities but not so small that the diligent eye of the proprietor had failed to notice.

When I asked, Cyril said he had given keys to both the assistant, Adrian, and his granddaughter, Kirsty but couldn't rule out the possibility that there were other keys out there as he hadn't changed the lock since he bought the building. What I had spotted when I looked around the premises, was that the back door had a deadbolt on it so could only be opened from the inside. The windows were fitted with steel bars but the main entrance door was opened using a key. If a person wanted to break in, they could probably kick the door clean off its hinges. It was both old and made from wood in a wooden frame. I doubted it would take me long to defeat. However, there had been no forced entry. The invisible person had to be using a key and was using spearmint chewing gum to gum up the clapper in the bell each night. I had tasted a faint trace of it earlier and had found a wad of it on the clapper when I had Cyril let me in this evening.

I had no guarantee that Cyril's thief would make an appearance tonight but on balance of probability, unless they had a hidden camera alerting them to my presence in the shop, they would show up to make their nightly collection and if not tonight, then surely tomorrow night. I didn't want to do this for days but doubted I would have to.

At very nearly 0215hrs, with my bottom going numb from sitting still and quiet in the dark, the CCTV camera switched itself off. This had to have been achieved by a remote from outside the shop. I leaned forward to press a button on the control panel and watched as the monitor screen came back to life. I was filming again and the intruder had no idea.

Then, I heard the unmistakeable sound of a key turning in the lock outside.

In the darkness of the back office, I slowly stood up and twisted a little in place to unkink my back. On the camera, the front door to the shop opened and a figure slipped inside. Even in the dark, where the screen took on the appearance of an old black and white movie, I could tell the intruder was a man. The CCTV was recording everything as he moved around the shop tucking a packet of biscuits, a four-pack of beer and a bunch of bananas into a shopping basket as if he were going about his daily shop.

In preparation for what was to come, I put a small torch up to my right eye and shone it in while cupping my hands to limit the light leaking out. Then I waited for him to get well away from the front door and burst through from the back office to the shop, whacked the light switches as I went to blind the intruder and leaped the counter to land behind him. I was almost blind in one eye as it adjusted to the sudden light, but the one I had shone the torch into was no longer dilated and could take the bright light – I could see and he could not.

Adrian swung around to face me, blinking, confused and terrified. Then said, 'Aaaaaargh!' in a surprisingly high-pitched voice.

'Hello, Adrian. I'm Tempest Michaels and you're busted.' I delivered my lines triumphantly but hadn't expected the shopping basket which he swung in a scything upwards arc to uppercut my jaw. In retrospect, I think it was a fear-driven reaction to the black-clad figure suddenly appearing, but it smacked hard under my chin and knocked me over backward.

He was running for the door before I hit the floor. Somehow, despite tumbling backward out of control, I still manged to snag his right foot as he tried to get by me. I didn't need to apprehend him, I had enough footage to ensure a conviction but for completeness I didn't think that letting the criminal escape was a good practice.

Adrian's foot tried to break free only to find my grip was superior to his determination. This resulted in his forward momentum taking his centre of gravity beyond the point of balance and inevitably he fell flat on his face. He continued to kick and fight though, desperately trying to break free.

'Adrian, it's too late. There is nowhere to run away to. You might as well relax.' I was trying to reason with him, but he wasn't inclined to listen. In fact, he was borderline hysterical, and I was starting to get worried that he might hurt himself. I bunched my muscles, leaping from my position on the floor onto his back where I was instantly able to pin him down. It was safer for both of us. With my left hand between his shoulder blades and my knees on his rump, my superior weight and strength stopped him from getting up. After a few seconds of trying to throw me off, he accepted defeat and gave up. Then I spotted a small rectangular lump in the back of his jeans. Reaching into his back-right pocket, I slid out a little remote control. It bore the same manufacturers name as the CCTV control unit and explained how he had been turning it on and off.

'Adrian!' Cyril's voice cut through the quiet like a claxon signalling the end of a round, 'It was you?' Cyril's voice carried a level of disappointment that would have crippled me if I had ever heard it from my father. I turned to see Cyril's face, I swear the heartbreak etched on to it would stay with me for the rest of my life.

It had the same effect on Adrian as it did on me. All the struggle went out of him under the terrible sadness that emanated from Cyril. Cyril flapped his arms a few times. He was trying to find something to say and struggling to find the words. 'I don't understand, Mr Michaels. I thought it was my granddaughter. What would Adrian want with tampons?'

'Adrian, would you like to field that question?' I asked. When he said nothing, I answered for him, 'The thefts started after Kirsty started working here. I think Adrian saw an opportunity to throw suspicion elsewhere and I expect his house is filled with stolen goods.' Still kneeling on Adrian's back, I looked at Cyril with a serious face. 'It's time to call the police, Cyril.'

Cyril's face swung to look at mine while beneath me, Adrian said, 'The police?'

I shot him a look that shut him up, then turned back to Cyril. 'There is no choice if you wish to press charges.'

He nodded reluctantly, turned around and went back into the office. Adrian looked at me and moved as if he was going to get up. I shot him a single eyebrow raise as a warning and held it until he accepted the futility of resistance and settled back onto the linoleum floor.

A minute later, Cyril wandered back out, 'They will be here in a few minutes,' he announced. I simply nodded and watched as Cyril walked to the counter, reached over and produced a bottle of brandy. He pulled the cork from it with his teeth, spat it out and took a healthy slug. He didn't turn around but his whole body gave an involuntary shudder.

Thankfully, only a few minutes of uncomfortable silence had to be endured before flashing light began to illuminate the darkness outside. The police were here already. I turned to Cyril, 'What you do next is your choice. Adrian has broken into your shop and stolen from you. There is now video footage which is still running and has recorded all of tonight's events. It can be used by the police and I will attend any interviews and a court case if necessary. I will send you an invoice for my services in the next couple of days. Is there anything else you need me to do?'

'I would just like to get this finished and get to bed, if that's alright, Mr Michaels,' said Cyril.

I checked my watch: 0257hrs. 'I don't appear to have anything further to do, mystery solved and all, so getting to bed sounds good to me as well.' We stood for a moment just staring at each other waiting for someone to speak.

If it lasted any longer it was going to be weird and he was clearly waiting for me to say something. I gave a sort of "I'm off" motion with one hand. 'You have my number if you need me. Good evening to you.' I gave him a cheery smile and headed into the night, but I didn't get as far as I wanted because the police were right outside, and wouldn't you know it? It was the same two cops that had arrested me a few hours ago.

'You have got to be kidding me,' said the man whose name I still hadn't learned. He had widened his stance so he could block my route. Clearly, he thought he was here to arrest me as he reached behind his back to grab his baton. He flicked it expertly so it extended to its full length of about three feet and held it up in a gesture intended to threaten me into submission.

'Good morning,' I greeted them both with more volume and gusto than the situation required. I had no intention of going through any more nonsense with them, so I put out my hand for it to be shaken. 'Tempest Michaels, private investigator.' It was what it said on my business card, but it didn't fit my activities. 'The chap you want is inside.' I turned to wave to Cyril who was still stood on the doorstep, his expression shocked from the exchange he was watching. 'That's my client, Mr Martelle.'

'Okay,' Debbie said slowly. 'You're going to have to come back inside with us though until we get this straightened out.'

I thought about it for a second, trying to see it from their point of view and decided that I probably had very little choice. I smiled back at the two uniformed officers and said, 'Jolly good,' as I turned and went back inside again.

Frank's Bookshop. Friday, March 19th 1127hrs

I HAD SLEPT IN this morning, giving myself a chance to actually rest since it was 0413 when I finally got to bed. The dogs had been pleased to see me though I could never tell if they were bothered I was out or relieved to see me as they always displayed the same level of exuberant excitement whether I had been gone minutes or hours. They had needed a trip to the garden but were otherwise ready to climb into bed with me, their designated sleeping place of under the bed never enticing enough when they knew they could share my bed each night.

At least someone did.

Upon rising, they had decided they were hungry, which, to be fair, is a default setting they come preloaded with. It was dry out and the frost I could see in a few places still in the shade had been chased away by the advancing sun to leave the early spring morning pleasantly warm. The three of us had embarked on a long walk around the village where country paths lead through vineyards and corn fields as they rise to the north up the side of Bluebell Hill. From the high point I reached about halfway up the slope, I could see so far into the distance that the horizon could be seen curving away on each side.

I could have left the dogs sleeping in the house after our walk but elected to take them with me to see what they thought of the new office. In my ideal world I would be able to have them with me more often than not. I couldn't take them to meet clients or on stakeouts if such things became regular, but I could have them in the office.

On today's list of tasks was a conversation with Richard Claythorn. I had met his stalker last night, although met would probably not be the right term. In giving chase though, I proved his existence and wanted to tell him about the peep hole I had found. I doubted J would return to that spot, so I was a little flummoxed regarding my next move. Richard had provided me with letters and emails from J yesterday, but I had not found time to do more than casually glance at them until this morning while I walked the dogs. J failed to reveal his name in any of the correspondence but the tone had been genuinely friendly as if he were writing fan mail or exchanging letters with a friend. Each was signed to Rich from your old pal J. However, the genuinely friendly tone didn't last and the most recent one, which was three months ago, was short and terse.

Rich,

Your continued refusal to respond to my requests has forced my hand. I must escape my bounds and flee directly to you. We must join as brothers and packmates. With me as your Beta, you will rule the night once more.

I'll be with you soon.

Your old pal

J

It was clear he was talking about being a werewolf and wanted Richard to play the role of Alpha in a pack he would lead. This much though had been explained by Richard right at the start of the case. I couldn't tell if the man was dangerous but watching him pretend to transform into a werewolf last night had convinced me he was delusional. His appearance was troubling too. When he had stared at me, he looked just like a werewolf. His face had not been that of a human, but he had escaped me so how the effect was achieved remained a mystery.

'Come on, chaps,' I called as I collected my keys and pocketed my phone. I was heading to Rochester and the office and they were coming with me. Of course, they had just walked three miles on tiny legs and had no intention of leaving their comfortable position on the sofa. The sun, when it shone, lit the sofa in the afternoon to make it warm and they could reliably be found there basking in its rays. Right now, they had assumed the position the sun would first hit and I had to pick them up and carry them out of the house to make sure they came with me. Had I put them down inside the house, they would each have ducked around my legs and run back to beat the other to the best spot.

In the car, I ran through more ideas about how J had created the werewolf appearance. A mask was the answer that presented itself as most likely. He had the time to slip it on when he had crouched down. I had lost sight of him briefly at that point.

I wonder what Frank would say.

The thought caught me by surprise. The odd little bookshop owner I met yesterday had been pleasant enough, but I had doubted I would ever see or speak to him again. Now I was considering whether he might be a resource to call upon. As I parked the car, it was toward his shop that I walked, not my office.

I didn't know where it was exactly, just its general location. He said it was just around the corner from my office and had waved a hand in the direction of the bridge. That was where I looked, but there was no sign of it. Only when I gave up looking, did I spot a door that seemed to lead nowhere. On Northgate, a short road leading away from the castle, was a nondescript open door. The poster inside had drawn my eye. It was a classic fuzzy UFO picture I had seen dozens of times in my life. No doubt it was some famously faked picture, but the door led to stairs which I could see ascending to the right and as my eye tracked up, I saw a sign sticking out from the wall claiming the premises to be The Mystery Men bookshop.

There were more pictures on the walls going up the stairs: The Loch Ness Monster, a movie poster from Aliens. There was a definite theme.

A bell jingled as I went inside, the dogs pulling excitedly to get there first even though they had no idea where we were going.

The inside of the bookshop, for that was clearly what it was, contained more than just books. High wooden bookshelves ran all the way around the room and there were three rows of them back to back across the room, but there were also glass display cabinets in which figurines could be seen. I recognised ED-209 from Robocop and a model of the Sulaco from Aliens. More posters from movies and prints of mythical beasts adorned the walls and by the counter, a whole rack of comic books. I was the only customer in the shop but behind the counter, a short, pretty oriental girl had looked up from the graphic novel she was reading.

'They aren't going to pee on anything are they?' she asked, looking at the dogs.

'I don't expect them to,' I replied.

My answer seemed good enough for her. 'Help you?' she asked as she stood up properly to show me that she had on a sports bra beneath the thin, open sweater she had on. She was very toned and athletic like a professional athlete or someone that takes martial arts classes seriously.

I moved further into the shop, approaching the counter. 'I'm looking for Frank?' I asked. 'Sorry, I don't know his last name.'

The girl had a name badge pinned to her sweater. I hadn't seen it until she turned slightly to yell through the door behind her. It said Poison on it.

From the door that led off behind the counter, I heard footsteps approaching and then the scrawny, odd little man I had met yesterday swung into view. As he came to rest next to the girl, my brain made a note that the two people in front of me were a study in genetics and how some won and some lost. Poison was physical perfection, although if I had to guess I would say she was still in her teens, where in contrast Frank was a physical misfire. He was older than me, maybe even pushing forty and shorter even than I remembered from yesterday. Like yesterday he was smiling broadly.

'Oh, Mr Michaels, so good to have you in the shop. What brings you to our fine establishment this day?'

I licked my lips and composed the question I had but couldn't quite believe I was going to ask, 'I took Richard Claythorn's case. He has a stalker and is worried the person might intend him some harm. The individual in question has been spying on him but gave me the slip last night, although not before I watched him pretend to transform into a werewolf. I was hoping you might be able to...'

'Help you with some information?' Frank finished my sentence. 'That is what I am here for, Mr Michaels. Poison, would you fetch Gunther's Guide to Lycanthropic Beasts, please?' he said as he turned to face his assistant. As she scurried away to comply, he turned back to me, 'Now what sort of werewolf was it?'

I gave him my best single eyebrow lift. 'A fake one?'

'No, I mean was it a loup-garou or a lycanthrope?'

I just stared at him unsure what possible response I could be expected to have.

He saw my confusion but didn't expand any further. Instead, he paused for a second until Poison brought a large and very old-looking book from the back room. She was wearing gloves and had a second pair for Frank to put on. 'It's four hundred years old,' he explained. Expertly, he opened the book to a page he wanted then turned it carefully so it faced me. There were drawings of different types of werewolf.

'Like that one,' I said, pointing to a drawing of a man with a bare torso and trousers on his legs. His face was distorted to look like a wolf but only sort of like a wolf.

Frank nodded his understanding, 'A loup-garou. Okay,' he closed the book and handed it back to Poison as he slipped off his gloves. 'In many ways this is good news.'

'How so?' I asked, truly curious to hear what the crazy man had to say.

'Many consider the loup-garou to be the least dangerous of all the werewolf breeds and the easiest to kill. No silver bullet required thankfully. Removing the head or burning the creature will be sufficient to ensure the beast does not return. The same danger of being bitten and turned exists though. Tell me? Do you have a plan for tackling it? The full moon is tonight, after all.'

I really wasn't sure what to say. I was quite content that I had seen nothing more than a man with a werewolf fetish last night. I needed to corner him again and then see what I could do about getting charges against him for stalking. If I had been up against a werewolf, surely, he would not have run away as he had. Was I wasting my time attempting to explain that to Frank though?

In the end, I thought it best to be honest, 'Frank, the chap I chased last night was just a guy with a mask.' Actually, I didn't know it was a mask but I felt fairly certain that would be the case. 'What I need to do is work out how to find him or how to work out who he is. I guess I have research to do. Thank you for the help and advice though.' I thought for a second, 'Actually, do you have a book of werewolf lore I can buy? I think it might help to understand the man's motivation if I know more about werewolves.'

'Well, that is something I can certainly help you with. I also have all of Richard Claythorn's movies.'

And he did. I asked if any of them were any good but regretted the question when Frank launched into a long-winded explanation regarding the various elements of inaccuracy the movies promoted to enable their storylines. I stopped him though when he said that two of the movies were made in the local area. Kent being the historic area that it is, is littered with castles. Honestly, they are everywhere, so I guess I wasn't surprised to learn that a gothic fantasy werewolf movie and its sequel had been shot here.

I didn't want to buy the movies though, I had already bought all my combat gear and had a book on the counter in a bag ready to go. Frank though was almost offended by the suggestion that I should pay.

'Mr Michaels, it is the least I can do to assist you in your quest to rid the town of this foul beast. Please, borrow the movies and return them whenever. If I can be of any further service you need only ask.'

I thanked him, took my book and DVDs and a little bewildered, found myself back out in the sunlight in Rochester High Street wondering just what I should do next.

I hadn't been to the office in twenty-four hours, so I turned left and let the dogs lead me there. My business emails came to my phone, but they were less easy to read and reply to on it, whereas in the office I had a comfortable chair and a big screen with a keyboard.

As I tugged at the dogs leads because telling them to turn right wasn't having much effect, I fished out my keys and stopped in front of the door in the street. Above my head was a small sign that displayed the business name in bright blue letters against a white background. In my head I was going to have something snazzier. Maybe a neon sign that would look cool at night, however I had been trying to keep costs down and this had been cheap. I worried that it set the wrong tone, as might my simple business cards in that if they both looked cheap, then maybe I wasn't very good.

It was another thing to consider. At my feet, the little dogs were hopping with excitement as I opened the door. They were being taken somewhere new, though I could never know whether it was simply the opportunity to explore or the eternal hope that there might be food inside that propelled their enthusiasm. As I unclipped their leads, they both bounded forward, dashing up the stairs to find themselves faced by another door. That one wasn't locked though and in fact not even pulled shut as I saw them butt their way into with their heads.

Just as I reached the top step, my phone rang. Pulling it from my pocket, the screen displayed a familiar name, 'Hey, big feller. What's up?' I asked.

The caller was a guy called Benjamin Winters that I had met in the army. He and I had been assigned to the same unit and had served in war zones, trading shots and fighting alongside one another more than once. In such things strong bonds are formed. Coincidence placed the piece of England we each called home within a couple of miles of each other and now that we were both retired from that life, we met semi-regularly for a drink or a round of golf. His circumstances were vastly different to mine though. Where I needed a job to pay my bills, Big Ben had received a healthy insurance pay-out when his parents were tragically killed on the road due to negligence on the part of a national haulier. Now he lived the life of a playboy, aided by the money, but mostly driven by being the most handsome, most stunningly tall and muscular man you have ever met.

I hated him.

I didn't, of course. He was a great friend, but I couldn't deny the envy each time I saw him with yet another beautiful woman and I went home to cuddle a dog.

'Hey, knob jockey,' Big Ben was such a delight, 'Do you have lunch plans?'

My stomach rumbled at the question. 'No, I do not.' My breakfast had been a banana and was long forgotten.

'Cool,' he replied. 'I just finished a round of golf so I'm passing Rochester. You opened your business yesterday didn't you?'

I indulged myself with an eyeroll. I knew that sooner or later I was going to have to tell people about the error in the paper, but where some might offer a word of sympathy, I would not get that from my friends and certainly not from Big Ben who was always first in the queue to exchange banter.

'Yes, I did,' I replied, 'I have several cases already and solved one last night in fact.'

'Wow. That was fast work. You're at the office, right?'

'Yup.'

'See you in ten minutes.' Then he hung up.

During the brief exchange I had time to put my bags down and power up the computer which was now blinking its cursor at me and waiting for something to do. I navigated to the email icon: sixty-three new emails.

A quick sift eliminated more than half of them. They were spam: offers to enlarge my penis through the use of magic pills, adult dating sites and other rubbish. I had to wonder what I might have clicked on in the past to have warranted such communication. There were genuine enquiries though, ones which I probably should have read and responded to already.

freindlyfish@grabmail.co.uk. The email was even signed off by Freindly Fish so I couldn't tell whether I should respond with Dear Sir or Dear Madam, but since the content of the email reported that their cat had been possessed and was trying to kill them, I elected to press delete.

Suzie37@britnet.com reported that her boss was practising devil worship and she believed he was grooming his teenage niece to be used as a sacrifice. However, once I had read the rest of the email, I suspected that she was in fact upset about not getting a promotion and was making the whole thing up. I filed it away to consider later. The remaining emails were similar in that they were all offers to pay me money but also utter nonsense. There were four different requests for me to rid people of an evil presence in their house, two of them describing a cold sensation they always felt in a particular spot which I was certain would prove to be next to a window or an air vent. I also had two enquiries with dates they wanted me to perform at a child's party and one request to perform an exorcism. The stupid advert had only been out for two days.

The bottom door opened just as I pressed send on my response to the final email. 'You up there, Tempest?' called Big Ben.

I called back, 'Come on up.'

Stomping feet on wooden steps preceded his big, daft head appearing around the doorframe, 'Hey, Mike Hammer,' he said as he came in, the boys fussing around him, 'or are you more Columbo?'

'At least you didn't lead with Miss Marple.'

'Dang it. Missed a chance there,' he laughed. 'So how did the first day go? You were worried you might not get any calls but you said you solved a case already? What was it? Missing glasses that you found on the person's face?' He was having a great time entertaining himself.

Trying hard to not roll my eyes, I decided to tell him the truth and see what he made of it, 'It was an invisible man.'

He waited a second for the punchline, then realised none was coming. His forehead crinkled a little while he considered my statement. 'An invisible man. Isn't that a little unusual for a private detective?'

I pushed my chair back from the desk and explained about the mistake in the paper, the calls and emails I had received and all about the werewolf I had chased and the invisible thief I had caught last night.

Big Ben had laughed so hard I worried he might wet himself or suffer a hernia. 'And you got arrested!' he spluttered, 'Wait until I tell the guys.'

'Are we getting lunch?' I asked, feigning impatience but genuinely hungry.

'Yeah, I'm buying,' he said. 'This is the most fun I have had since last night.'

I knew better than to ask what happened last night. Big Ben went through women at an alarming rate so last night had probably involved three redheads and a jar of peanut butter or something like that.

'What's with the old movies?' he asked, pointing to the two DVDs on my desk.

I had stood up and was putting things into my pockets to leave. 'They are to do with a case I am working now. The lead actor in these movies has a stalker that thinks he is a werewolf. That's who I chased last night.'

'Really?'

'Really.'

He picked up the two DVDs to scrutinise. 'Richard Claythorn. I remember him.'

'You do? I had never heard of him.'

He shrugged. 'My dad liked his films. There was always an abundance of naked women in them. I expect these are the same. Are you planning to watch them?'

'Just for research.'

'Sounds good,' he said as he headed for the door, the two film cases in one giant hand. 'Let's get lunch to go and watch one this afternoon. I just had a new home cinema fitted.'

I said, 'Okay,' after a moment's pause. I couldn't think of a reason why I shouldn't.

Movies. Friday, March 19th 1403hrs

BIG BEN APPEARED TO enjoy the first film. We planned to watch both of them one after the other, burning through almost three and a half hours while the dogs slept on the couch between us. Big Ben had a penthouse apartment on the top floor of a building inside a gated community that overlooked the river Medway as it ran through Maidstone town centre. That made the location sound nicer than it was, but the apartment itself was highly desirable and spacious. His cinema room was exactly that: a separate room with a couple of couches and a huge screen TV with surround sound. The eighties movies we were watching didn't have the Dolby sound recording that would allow us to appreciate it, but it was still the best way to watch them.

I found the films boring, predictable, poorly acted and dated, which Big Ben said was part of the allure.

The plot of the first film, Bite of the Werewolf was pretty thin: Man (played by Richard Claythorn) gets bitten, man turns into werewolf, man joins pack and fights to become the alpha while around him the cast take their clothes off and have sex or kill people with horrific, yet still very B movie, effects. One of the only points of interest was that it had all been shot in the local area. It was an Elstree Studios film and Kent was littered with castles as I may have mentioned before, so finding gothic looking castles to act as a backdrop had probably been quite easy though I couldn't work out which one I was looking at.

The Alpha werewolf that Richard Claythorn's character was trying to depose as leader was played by someone I thought looked familiar. As the film progressed, I became increasingly curious about where I knew him from. I was guessing that it was some other film I had watched at some point though I could not join the dots to dredge the memory to the surface.

Then, on the screen the mystery actor began changing into a werewolf. I sat bolt upright, almost ejecting Dozer from my lap as I did.

'You alright, mate?' asked Big Ben.

'Who is that actor?'

'Which one?'

I pointed to the screen, trying to form a coherent sentence that would articulate my thoughts. Frustrated with my swiss-cheese brain, I took out my phone to use the search engine.

And there was the answer to the case. The actor's name was Jay Jeffries. Reading his name, I knew instantly that the place I knew his face from was the shaft of moonlight last night as he stood by the fence pretending to change into a werewolf. Watching him act out the transformation into werewolf was something I had watched in person less than twenty-four hours ago. He had just done it exactly the same on the TV.

Big Ben had paused the film to see what I was doing. I showed him the image on my phone. 'This is the guy I chased last night. He's the client's stalker. The letters and emails he wrote were all signed with a J; his name is Jay Jeffries.'

'Case solved then.'

'Not exactly,' I was thinking as I was speaking. 'Knowing who he is doesn't get me anywhere. The task is to force him to stop stalking the client or to prevent him from taking it a stage further and harming him, if that is his intention.'

'Ok,' said Big Ben, rolling his shoulders, 'let's find him and ask him nicely to stop.' When he said nicely, he mimed strangling a person with one hand while hitting him repeatedly with the other.

I shook my head, 'We have to stay within the bounds of the law.'

'Or we might get arrested,' he laughed.

I performed an involuntary eye roll. I wasn't going to hear the end of that for some time. 'I need a computer. I need to find this guy.'

We left the cinema room, the Dachshunds making grumpy noises as we moved them but neither finding the energy to follow us. In the main living room, Big Ben had a white marble desk on which was positioned an Apple Mac. It had to be the biggest one they made, a demonstration of how much money Big Ben had at his disposal. I had a smaller version at home. Big Ben indicted that I should crack on and asked if I wanted a coffee.

While I tried to wheedle information from the internet, he made hot beverages, the sound of a coffee machine getting excited coming unseen from the kitchen.

Jay Jeffries had a Wikipedia page and a few other entries under google but no social media presence whatsoever. The wiki page confirmed that he had been an actor, but his career had been even more limited than Richard's. Bite of the Werewolf wasn't the only movie it listed but it was the last and it didn't say why he had never worked after that. I tried a few other searches but didn't find anything much until I typed in *Jay Jeffries+family* at which point I found a sister.

A further ten minutes of digging through LinkedIn, Facebook and other sites told me where she worked, from which I found a website and discovered she was a Director of the business which in turn allowed me to interrogate Companies House to get her home address. I used that and her name to get a phone number via online phone services. Big Ben had gone for a shower, getting it done now because he was going out soon. Friday night was typically pub night at the local alehouse in my village. All the other guys already lived there, it was just Big Ben that had to travel but since he didn't like to go more than a day without having sex, he generally had to hurry home at closing time because he had a girl about to arrive at his place

He was in his bedroom now getting dressed, some kind of party anthems CD playing loud to get him in the mood for going out. I went back into his cinema room and closed the door to shut the worst of the noise out so I could make the call.

Jay Jeffries's sister answered on the first go, 'Hello.'

'Good afternoon. My name is Tempest Michaels, I'm a private investigator and I have a case that I believe may involve your brother. Can I trouble you to answer a couple of questions?'

She didn't say anything for a few seconds making me think she was about to hang up but then I heard the distinctive sound of a cigarette being lit. 'I don't know where he is, if that is what you are about to ask me.'

'Well, that is information I am interested to gain but actually I was hoping you could tell me a bit more about him. Can you tell me if he knew Richard Claythorn, he was an actor...'

'Yeah, I know who he was,' she cut in over me. 'He had an affair with Jay's wife. He and Jay were best friends for a while, but when he found out about that... well, let's just say his life went downhill from there.'

A big piece of the puzzle slotted into place. Jay or J as he signed his letters was well known by my client and I knew now why Jay was stalking him. Why now though? 'What exactly do you mean by went downhill please? Can you elaborate?' I asked.

I heard her take a long drag on her cigarette, 'Jay hit the bottle. His career ended almost overnight. His stupid wife even tried to come back when she found out Richard had no interest in her, but Jay didn't care by then. He became depressed, tried to take his own life a bunch of times and his mental health carried on deteriorating until he was sectioned. That was more than fifteen years ago and he had been in hospitals and care centres ever since. I gave up trying to communicate with him years ago.'

'Why is that?' I was scribbling notes as fast as I could.

'Because he became delusional. He thinks he is a werewolf. He howls at night and they have to sedate him because he tries to bite and claw the doctors and orderlies. Three... no nearly four weeks ago he escaped from a ward in a specialist care unit in Canterbury. I found out because I am still listed as his emergency contact, but he's not going to contact me, and I wouldn't help him if he did.'

'Why is that, please?' I asked the same question again.

Another long drag on her cigarette and then an expletive as she started talking again, 'It's his fault I got no inheritance. Mum said he needed it more. To make sure he was taken care of. I didn't get a damned penny.'

Jay's sister continued to rant for a while longer but had no more details that were of use. Jay's wife had also been an actress, but she had no idea where she might be now. When I ended the call, I knew who the stalker was and what was motivating him. I also knew that the client had brought it on himself. Not that it made a difference to my case, but it gave context. As did the fact that Jay Jeffries was probably dangerous: They had to sedate him because he tried to bite and claw people.

Then I remembered the letters he had written. The theme throughout had been the desire to have Richard join his pack. He wanted Richard to be the Alpha to his Beta. How would he achieve that? Did he plan to bite him? Was he more dangerous than that? Would he kill Richard in a frenzied attack as revenge for his failed marriage or for refusing to play werewolves with him? One thing that was bothering me was the likelihood that Richard had known the identity of the stalker all along. I had managed to work out who it was after catching a brief glimpse of his face in the moonlight, but Richard said he had spoken to him.

I had to call my client and ask a few questions. His phone rang off though and went to voicemail. I tried again with the same result. Maybe I could go to the house. I checked my watch: 1557hrs. I went to look for Big Ben.

He was talking on the phone, quite clearly to a lady since he was using his husky, come to bed tone. I waited for him to finish.

'I need to go check on my client,' I said as I hitched my bag onto my shoulder and called for the dogs, 'I know who the stalker is and why he is stalking my client. I just need to catch him now.'

'Okay. You're pretty good at this, aren't you? Detective stuff.' I shrugged. I had only solved one case so far. 'Will you stick with the paranormal thing? Make it a specialty?'

'Goodness, no,' I shook my head vigorously, 'No, I just need to get that advert straightened out and then I can go after normal cases.'

Big Ben considered that for a second. 'That doesn't sound anywhere near like as much fun. See you at the pub?'

'Sure thing. You want me to leave the DVDs for you to watch?'

'Nah. I'll be too busy starring in my own movies,' he said making a gesture that made it abundantly clear what sort of movies he was planning to make later.

With the dogs in tow, I went back to my car and set off to ask the client why he had lied about knowing who his stalker was.

Missing Client. Friday, March 19th 1627hrs

TRAFFIC WAS PICKING UP on the way out of Maidstone. Bluebell Hill, which dominated the landscape, was also the main artery that led from the city to two different motorways and the towns between and beyond. It was choc-full of cars at this time of day, but I had to use it to get where I wanted to go. The additional traffic meant the short journey from Big Ben's apartment to Richard's house took twice as long as it otherwise might have and I called him twice more while I was stuck in traffic, getting the same result as before.

It was still daylight, so I wasn't worried that something might have happened to him until I got to his house and found the front door unlocked. I called Chatham police station and asked for PC Debbie McHardy. I had no idea if she was going to be there, but she was, and although it took almost a minute before she picked up the phone, I was relieved to have reached someone I could speak to without having to spend ten minutes trying to explain who I was.

'McHardy,' she answered, professional boredom in her voice.

'Good afternoon, this is Tempest Michaels.'

'Ohhhhh,' she drawled, 'the ghost catcher. What are you up to this time? Wait, did you call to get my number?' she was teasing me, my call clearly unwelcome, as if it had disturbed from something far more important like her coffee break.

I answered without reacting to her sarcasm, 'Debbie I think my client might be missing. His front gate and front door are unlocked and...'

'Well, we'll get right on it. Hold on while I call the Chief of Police.'

'Debbie, his car is not in his garage,' I had peered through the window, 'and his house has been left open.' I kept my voice even and calm.

'So, he went out and forgot to lock up. People do it all the time. Don't sweat it.'

'Really, Debbie?'

'That's PC McHardy to you,' she replied snippily.

'Debbie,' I persisted, 'I am reporting that a man with a known stalker has gone missing. Less than twenty-four hours ago, I reported that I had chased a man from the perimeter of the man's property and now I am calling to say the man's where-abouts are unknown. Are you seriously going to do nothing?'

There was silence for a few seconds which I took to be PC McHardy wondering if perhaps she wasn't walking her self into a trap if my client did turn out to be in trouble. Eventually she said, 'If you have a missing person to report, please come to the station and report it,' then she hung up on me.

I gave my phone an accusing stare. Help from the police would not be coming. I tapped my foot and wondered what my next move should be. I had no easy way of locating Richard and wasn't sophisticated enough to be able to track him by his phone. It was entirely possible he wasn't answering the phone for a good reason. He might be at the cinema or with a lady or at a funeral. I had no way of knowing, so while my gut wanted to believe he was in trouble, I had to accept that I didn't know what to do about it.

My watch told me it was 1648hrs. The sun was dipping behind the trees of Bluebell Hill, throwing long shadows across the pavement as the darkness crept in. Flummoxed by my lack of options, I slid back into the car where my two madly tail-wag-ging Dachshunds jumped across the transmission tunnel to nuzzle me on the driver's seat. I petted them, then lifted them over to the passenger side one at a time and started back toward my house. They would want their dinner soon and it was a task I actually knew how to perform.

Pub O'clock. Friday, March 19th 1847hrs

SINCE I WAS UNSURE what I could do for my client's case that would be productive, I got a shower and made some food. My routine was such that I almost always went to the pub in the village on a Friday night. It was a routine that had started while I was in the Army, Friday nights often being legendary events at whatever unit I was stationed at in whatever part of the world. I had been serious about the fitness aspect of my career so had generally limited drinking alcohol to that one night and limited my drinking on that night to that which I could reasonably handle. I knew it was counterproductive to my hours in the gym and on the track, but I also recognised that camaraderie in such an environment was important and there were few places better for bonding than the bar.

Now that I was a civilian, the practice of drinking on a Friday night continued, and I liked that I had an old brother in arms that came along with me most weeks. At 1847hrs I had shackled the dogs and left the house to take a winding route to the pub. It was a dry evening though it was cool under the cloudless sky as I hurried the dogs to get their business and snuffling done so I could get my lips to a cold glass of amber liquid.

As I came back into the village having completed a loop through the vineyard to the north, my phone pinged to announce a text message arriving.

I'm at the bar, butt nugget, want your usual?

Big Ben was delightful as always. I replied that my estimated time of arrival was four minutes and yes to my usual, thank you. Walking through the village always made me feel warm and comfortable. I had done my service and survived it relatively unscathed. I had a few scars that were nothing to brag about, but the point was that after the noise, danger and general craziness of a military career, now I got to appreciate how quiet and relaxed my life was. I live in a small, well-tended village where life was always quiet. Under the street lamps my shadow seemed to dance from one pool of light to the next as I walked and around me houses were lit with families relaxing as parents came home for the start of the weekend. It was all very pleasing to observe.

The dogs knew our routine and liked the pub because I would feed them a packet of potato chips whenever we went in. As we drew near, they quickened their pace and pulled at their leads to get to their destination. Crossing the carpark, I caught sight of Big Ben inside.

Then my phone rang. I halted the dogs advance on the pub door thinking it would most likely be Richard Claythorn returning the many missed calls. It wasn't though. It was a landline number, a local one, but not one I recognised. Since it might be another client calling with an enquiry, I answered, 'Blue Moon Investigations, Tempest Michaels speaking.'

'Mr Michaels, this is PC McHardy. It would seem I owe you an apology,' she sounded genuinely remorseful.

'Go on,' I encouraged wondering what had sparked the call.

She cleared her throat. 'Richard Claythorn's car has just been found abandoned.' The news hit me like a slap to the face. Here I was about to go out drinking when my client was in trouble, 'There was signs of a struggle and a small amount of blood.'

'Can you tell me anything else?' I asked.

'Not at this time. I thought you should know, that's all.'

I sensed that she was about to end the call and I really wanted some more detail, 'Can you at least tell me where the car was found?'

'On the B526 near Motely Cross. I haven't seen it, I am just relaying the information. I have to go,' and yet again she hung up on me.

I tapped my phone to my lips a few times, trying to make a decision. I didn't have to think about it for long though. Jay Jeffries had taken Richard by force. I was certain of it and I didn't need to know the details to know that I needed to act.

Motely Cross was fifteen miles away, no distance at all, but the police were already where the car was. So, where were Richard and Jay?

'Get off the phone,' called Big Ben. He had seen me through the window and stuck his head out the door. 'The others are all on the way and your pint is getting warm.' The dogs were straining to get to the friendly person they knew would make a fuss of them, 'Hello, boys,' he said as he bent to give them a scratch on the ears. Then he glanced back up at me, he caught my expression and asked, 'What?'

What? It was good question. 'I think my client has been taken and is either about to be killed or seriously hurt by a man that thinks he is a werewolf and has a grudge against him.'

Big Ben just stared at me.

'I have to go. Tell the guys I'll see them next week.' I reeled the dogs in, apologising to them as I forced them to turn to face the opposite direction. I needed to get home, get my new combat gear on and work out where Jay might have taken my client.

'Wh... hold on, Tempest. Where are you going?' Big Ben asked, now leaving the pub and coming after me.

'Actually, I don't really know. My client's car was found over by Motely Cross. My best guess is they went on foot from there. I'm going home to grab a map and some gear and then I'm heading out that way to see if I can track him down.'

'I'm driving,' said Big Ben, pouring his pint away and producing his keys. Across the car park a huge, black, Ford utility vehicle's lights flashed. I couldn't come up with an argument, so we all piled in, the dogs going onto the back seat of the double cab as we slid in the front. 'There's a map in the tray under your seat.'

I fished it out and tried leafing through it as he weaved the car around the roads to get to my house. It wasn't far so getting there only took a few seconds, 'Wait here,' I yelled as I bailed out, plipped my car open and grabbed the bag from the boot. As we set off again, I asked, 'Are you sure you want to spend your Friday night chasing lunatics? Don't you usually have a few pints then go home and shag your latest piece of fluff?'

'Civilian life is boring, mate. I never get to hit anyone anymore,' and that seemed to be all he had to say on the matter.

Using a finger and the light above my head, I was trying to find a place on the map where Jay and Richard might be. It was a road map I was looking at though, not an ordnance survey map which would have shown churches and public houses and other details I might find useful. We were halfway there when I wondered if perhaps we hadn't been a bit too hasty.

'We might need to find a garage and buy a better map?' I said.

Big Ben glanced across at me, his face doubtful, 'Out here? You'll be lucky.'

He was right. Kent had lots of towns and cities, but it had far more rural villages all linked by winding B roads that could go for many miles between signs of civilisation. The B526 was one such road.

'Do we turn back?' he asked. 'We passed a gas station ten minutes ago. They might have one.'

'No let's keep going. The cop I spoke with said his car was found on this road. They won't have had time to move it yet so we can stop and find out what they know.'

Sure enough, five minutes later we could see flashing blue lights bouncing off the trees half a mile ahead. We didn't get there though as Big Ben slammed his brakes on and brought the car to a halt.

I shot him a questioning look, but he was already in reverse, turned in his seat to look out his rear window. I respected him enough to stay quiet and wait for him to explain. He reached up to extinguish the light above my head as once again he brought the car to a standstill.

In the headlights was a tourist signpost, one of the brown ones with white writing and symbols on it to show tourists there was a point of interest nearby. This one said Motely Castle and had an arrow pointing left.

Confused, I said, 'Okay,' in response to Big Ben pointing excitedly at the sign like it should mean something.

He realised I wasn't connecting the dots, 'Motely Castle, mate,' he waited for me to understand what that meant, saw that I was clueless and told me anyway, 'It's where they filmed Bite of the Werewolf.'

Ding, ding, ding, we have a winner!

Big Ben was a genius. Why else would they be out here?

'Do I go in stealthy or with the lights on and fast as hell, so we surprise whoever is there and scare the pants off them?'

I gave it some thought. 'I think stealthy, I don't want to spook the guy and have him kill my client so he can escape or turn it into a hostage situation or something. I reckon we can sneak right up on them.'

Big Ben nodded, killed his lights and turned down the narrow road that would lead to the castle. It took a minute before our eyes began to adjust to the dark, but the clear sky and full moon meant there was plenty of light to see by. Within a minute we could see the outline of the castle on the horizon, a starry backdrop silhouetting it where it sat on the high ground the builders would have selected a thousand years ago.

'Close enough?' he asked as we drew to within three-hundred yards. He coasted to a stop, using the handbrake not the pedal so the brakes lights wouldn't come on to give away our position.

'Yeah. Let's check it out.' From my bag I pulled out my black combat gear.

'Whoa,' said Big Ben, 'Who'd you steal that from? Batman?'

I wiggled my eyebrows at him. 'I bought it yesterday. I needed something hardwearing for occasions such at this.'

'Well, I need to get a set just like it.'

'What for?' I asked assuming he intended it for a sex game of some sort.

'For doing this, dummy. You ain't big enough to be out here running around chasing bad guys by yourself. You need Big Ben to back you up.'

He was being a dick, but he made a good point; backup might be necessary sometimes. 'I'll tell you what. If you are going to be my back up when I need you, I will buy you a full rig. This one won't fit you though, because I am soooo small compared to you. You great lump. Now can we stop messing around and go look for my client?'

We slid out of the car, not closing the doors behind us because of the noise it would make in the silence of the countryside at night, then, sticking to the line of trees to our right, we made out way toward the castle ruins ahead.

It was game time.

Game Time.
Friday, March
19th 1942hrs

THERE WAS BARELY ANY noise at all as we crept toward the ruined castle that now dominated the landscape before us, only a vague rustling of the trees from the slight breeze and the sound of animals scurrying from our path. I thought I heard something following us more than once and had to dismiss the idea as ridiculous.

I must have passed Motely Castle dozens of times in my life; in the back of the car as a child, not noticing it because I was too busy fighting with my twin sister and more recently as I ventured out around the county by myself. This was the first time I had stopped to visit though. Maybe I would come back in the daylight with the dogs for a better look.

The dogs!

Remembering that the dogs were in the back of Big Ben's car hit me like an uppercut. Fear gripped me. How on earth had I forgotten them. I reached out to touch his arm, bringing him to a stop so I could speak with him quietly.

'What's up?' he asked in a whisper.

Whispering back at him I tried to convey the panic I was currently feeling, 'The dogs. We left them in the car and left the doors open.'

'Will they stay there?'

'Not a chance. I thought I could hear something following me a minute ago. I have to find them, or they will see a rabbit and be gone forever.' The dogs loved to chase rabbits. Originally bred for hunting badgers, their long bodies were perfect for following creatures into their underground burrows. If I didn't catch them right now, I might be out here for days trying to locate them.

We were almost at the castle, the excitement of the chase making my pulse rise as adrenalin got me ready for whatever was ahead. I didn't actually know that Jay and Richard were here of course, I was just guessing, but the hunch felt solid. I knelt to look for the dogs and began urgently calling for them, my voice little more than a whispered hiss that probably didn't carry very far but I saw a dark form moving toward me from the trees a few yards behind us and relief flooded into me as a second sausage-shaped dark blob appeared.

'Come on, chaps,' I called again, encouraging them to come to me. I would have to rush them back to the car, shut them in and rush back again while Big Ben waited for me. I didn't get the chance to do so though as just when they got within a couple of yards, an eerie, otherworldly howl split the night air.

'Owwww-woooooo.'

It felt like an urgent request that lasted several seconds but something wired into my little dogs' brains made them react. One second they had been about to reach my waiting hands, the next they were barking at the top of their lungs and running full pelt toward the castle, whipping under Big Ben's legs as they vanished into the night with me shouting after them.

Big Ben laughed, 'Shall we dispense with the stealthy approach then?'

I was already running, expletives forming a queue in my head as I blamed myself for the change in situation. How had I forgotten the dogs? I was too excited to think straight, that was the answer and I knew it. With Big Ben keeping pace beside me, we rounded the castle to the right following the path the dogs had taken. Just around the first corner the ruin of the ancient structure could be more clearly seen.

Where the front façade was almost all still in place, the wall on this side was mostly missing. It gave a view inside the wide-open expanse of the courtyard that would have been contained by the castle walls and an entry point to it. My eyes though were drawn to the werewolf stood on the raised rock plinth in the centre of the courtyard. The rock had to be part of the crumbled wall, but I recognised it instantly from the stupid film we had watched this afternoon. In the film it had been the focus for the final scene where Richard's character had finally killed Jay's character and ascended to be the Alpha werewolf. Before us, the roles were being reversed. Lit by the bright moon overhead, Jay was once again shirtless despite the frigid night air. He was wearing his werewolf mask and there at his feet was Richard. My client's hands were bound, and Jay was holding him by the throat with one hand. I didn't see a weapon so if Jay planned to kill him... well, in the film one werewolf had killed the other by biting off the other's head. I couldn't see how Jay might pull that off, but I didn't think hanging around to watch was a good policy.

Big Ben had paused as we scrambled over the wall, 'Um, Tempest? That's a werewolf,' he pointed out. I had to admit it looked convincing. With the mask on to change the appearance of his head and face, and the hairy torso he displayed, the creature ahead of us looked every inch a werewolf. My dogs had caught his attention now though. They couldn't get to him on the high rock, but they were barking incessantly, his focus on them not Richard. I wasn't hanging around for Big Ben if the scene had spooked him, but whatever fear he felt quickly passed. As he caught up to me again, he said, 'Let's go pick a fight with it.'

Here's a thing about Big Ben, yes, he is tall and muscular, but he is also one of those guys for whom violence is an artform. At six feet seven inches tall, he has limbs far longer than all but a very small percentage of the planet and he knew how to use them. Like me, he had many, many hours of fight training under his belt, but unlike me, he was good at it. Oh, I could handle myself, especially when pitched against persons that were not trained. Big Ben though was something else. I had seen him in action several times in my military days and would have to liken fighting him with trying to juggle angry sharks.

I was out of breath and my shouts were still being ignored by the excited Dachshunds as we finally got to them. Unlike the dogs, we could climb the rock to get to the two men on it and the werewolf saw the approaching danger. He released his grip on Richard's throat, his victim slumping to the rocky slab as Jay turned to face us.

He tilted his head back and howled again, this time the noise sounding plaintive and forlorn. At my feet the dogs started barking again but the confidence I had felt a few seconds ago began to seep away as I saw figures emerge from the shadows of the castle ruins all around us.

A fresh surge of adrenalin made my heart race as both Big Ben and I turned in place to take in the new danger.

'Hey, Tempest?' called Big Ben. 'I think this is about to get... hairy,' he sniggered.

An involuntary laugh escaped my lips. I counted no fewer than ten new werewolves. In all his letters Jay had referred to his pack. It wasn't hyperbole though. Each of them was shirtless and wearing a mask of similar design to Jay's.

I said, 'It looks like we are going to have to fight our way out of this,' which to Big Ben was a lot like taking off the safety switch.

He shouted out to address the men now advancing on our position, 'No biting, okay? Anyone bites me and they get a jolly good smack in the pants.'

There was no more time for words though as his advice galvanised the werewolves into action. They charged us, coming as one from many different directions. They would all arrive at the same time unless we changed the game. I was terrified for my little dogs, but I couldn't defend them and fight my way out at the same time so I focused on what I could do, grabbed Big Ben's arm and pulled him after me as I ran at three werewolves to my right. This offset the circle meaning those behind us would arrive later. It wasn't much as strategies went but it might be enough.

With three werewolves to our front, we closed the distance to meet with them. In my head, I was aiming to deal with the one on the left, pile driving a punch to his head using my momentum and then using his weight to pendulum myself around to get to the one in the middle. Big Ben might get there first but there were plenty more coming. However, just before I could enact that plan, the dogs exploded from between my legs and threw themselves at my intended target.

Finally breaking character, the werewolf spoke, 'Ah, get off!' as the dogs worried his trouser legs. He looked down at the menace below, taking his eyes off me at the wrong moment. I scythed a stiff hand into his forehead, snapping it back to bowl him over, then followed him down with a knee to his chest. I had done nothing to arrest my fall, so he got the full force of my body weight amplified by velocity. The breath whooshed from him in a most satisfying way. I spun my head

119

as I regained my feet, but the other two werewolves had met with Big Ben and now looked like they had said unkind things about a Volvo's mother and elected to stand in the road.

It was a blessing that the stupid werewolves hadn't thought it necessary to carry weapons. Had they done so, the outcome of the fight might have been very different, but it became quickly apparent that our opponents were no match. My dogs were still growling like mad things and pulling at the first werewolf's left trouser leg. He was too out of breath to fight them off so just lay there quite still but for one leg that was dancing spasmodically from their efforts.

'Go easy,' I said as I saw Big Ben line up a haymaker punch. Having closed quarters with them, I could see that the men looked poorly nourished and underweight. Their ribs were showing, and they moved sluggishly because they were cold. In less than a minute we had knocked every one of them to the ground and were surrounded by the fallen as they groaned weakly. They didn't try to get up though which left Jay Jeffries as the only werewolf standing. He was stood atop the rock still with the bound form of my client at his feet.

I looked over my shoulder at Big Ben, 'Would you be so kind as to call the police?'

'Sure,' he replied. He was slightly out of breath from excitement and exertion but pulled a phone from a back pocket, the light from it illuminating his face as he made the call.

I walked the few feet back to the rock, taking in the scene before me. Then I realised I could still hear my dogs bothering the poor man I had knocked down. 'Dogs! Enough,' I used my insistent voice, each dog pausing and raising its head to look at me. Neither actually let go the mouthful of trouser they had though as if it were a prize too great to release. Sighing, I reached into a pocket to retrieve the small bag of gravy bones I kept there. The familiar rustle of plastic was enough to get their attention, I soon had them both at my feet and was able to turn my attention back to the matter at hand, 'Mr Jeffries can I ask that you please come down? I would much rather avoid any further violence.'

He growled at me, a guttural noise that might have terrified a person if they didn't already know that the figure before them was a crazy homeless man with no shirt. I was blessed with that information but even if I hadn't been, I doubted I would indulge myself with feelings of fear. Big Ben just acted disinterested, leaning against the huge rock while he spoke to the police.

I turned my attention back to the werewolf, 'Mr Jeffries, this is your last warning. I would rather end this without having to restrain you.'

I thought for a second that he was going to surrender, but instead he spread his arms to show his claws as he tilted his head back to howl again. Then, from the surface of the rocky slab, Richard swung his legs in a wide determined circle. I had thought him to be incapacitated but he felled the werewolf in one go.

The howl that had just been starting, changed from a, 'Owww-woooo,' into an, 'Oh shiii,' and then stopped suddenly as he hit the rock with his shoulders and neck leading the way.

Then his limp form toppled over the back and crashed to the ground out of sight.

'Ben can you give Mr Claythorn a hand please?' Leaving him to get my client down, I jogged around the rock, climbing over smaller rocks to get to where the werewolf now lay. He had a nasty lump on his head, and he was out cold, but his pulse was steady and his breathing even.

Big Ben and Richard joined me while I was checking him over. 'Let me at him,' demanded Richard darting forward and looking ready to fight the now unconscious man.

I stood up in one fluid motion and got into his face, 'Why did you lie to me about his identity?'

'What?' Richard looked quite taken aback.

'You were friends once. You hurt him and he fell apart and you had me trying to catch your stalker when you knew who it was all along. Why is that?' I snapped out my question, my anger barely suppressed.

He flapped his mouth a couple of times, no sound coming out, but it wasn't long before he found his indignance, 'You can't talk to me like that. You work for me.' He raised a hand to poke me in the chest, but I grabbed it with my own before he could.

'I don't work for you,' I replied, my voice as calm as I could manage. Big Ben folded his arms and watched, glancing across at the other werewolves occasionally to make sure they weren't going anywhere. 'You contracted my services to investigate a case, but you lied about the circumstances and it almost got you killed. You are the bad guy here, not Jay Jeffries.'

'I am not!' he protested loudly.

'That man is homeless and mentally ill.'

'Yes, he should be locked up,' Richard snapped.

The sound of sirens in the distance could suddenly be heard as the message from Big Ben found its way from dispatch to the cops just up the road. The insistent noise drew closer and closer still until the flashing blue lights began to illuminate the castle ruins and surrounding trees. Then it shut off and the next sound was a series of car doors slamming shut. I could hear them shouting for any persons on the premises to make themselves known, their voices carrying easily on the silent night air.

I was still staring at my client with different emotions fighting for dominance. I selected apathy even though anger won the vote and turned away as the police found their way around the same side of the castle we had come.

Looking back, it must have been quite the scene they came across. There was a giant man holding a well-groomed but now dishevelled man in a suit by his collar. A man dressed in SWAT gear and all around them the fallen bodies of shirtless hairy chested werewolves. The police had on high visibility jackets and were carrying the sort of torch that can illuminate the moon if aimed correctly. They had entered the castle grounds at a determined jog but had then come to a jarring halt. Judging by their expressions, they were trying to work out what the heck they were seeing.

I took a step, ignored the one cop that had enough gumption to order me to stay still, stretched out an arm and plucked the werewolf mask from the top of the nearest man's head.

'We have some injured here,' I announced, 'We could do with some help.' Of course, the dogs chose that moment to attack the new people with the brightly coloured coats. Just as the police sergeant with them started issuing orders and they finally sprang into action, fanning out to advance on us, my two sausage shaped idiots pelted across the grass at them barking for all they were worth.

Calling for them to stop had as much impact as asking a teenager to listen to their parents. I gave up and turned around to talk to Richard again. So far as I was concerned the case was closed. I would bill him the hours I had devoted to his case and the expenses I had incurred and would send his invoice in the next couple of days. I didn't get to say any of that though. I saw shock forming on Big Ben's face and half a second later I was bundled to the ground from behind.

Startled, I lashed out with an elbow, but it was not a werewolf having one last go at me, it was the police, misunderstanding the situation again and tackling the wrong guy. It didn't help my cause that I had tried to fight him off because he now had a fat lip and his colleagues were coming for me and Big Ben.

They were looking for Richard Claythorn and we looked to have him captive.

Case Closed. Friday, March 19th 2019hrs

Who we were and what we were doing took some explaining. However, after thirty minutes and a call placed back to Chatham police station to speak with PC McHardy, who thankfully confirmed that she knew me and had alerted me about Richard's car, we were released. Richard had elected not to speak out to defend his saviours, which I think said a lot about the man. He was the kind of chap that would sleep with a friend's wife then discard her and not care about the lives he had ruined.

Ambulances had arrived to tend to the werewolves. They were half frozen and liable to suffer from hypothermia if they remained exposed plus they had injuries from their encounter with Big Ben. Jay Jeffries was still unconscious when they took him away. A reporter had arrived moments after the ambulance, an attractive woman with a shock of light red hair who, unsurprisingly, was very interested in the two men in custody. Her attempts to ask us questions were thwarted by the police but she didn't retreat far and I overheard that she had been at the scene down the road where they had found Richard's abandoned car. Richard had departed in a police car several minutes earlier when I think the uniformed officers could take no more of his whinging. He wasn't allowed his car back yet and that was upsetting him greatly. His Bentley convertible was evidence though and had to be duly processed before he could have it back.

When they finally took the cuffs off and let Big Ben and I out of the police car we had been stowed in, I asked, 'What will happen to them?' indicating the werewolves with my head.

The cop looked surprised by my question, but answered it anyway, 'They're all homeless it seems. The, ah... the unconscious man?'

'Jay Jeffries,' I supplied.

'Yeah him. He apparently gave them all money and promised them food and somewhere to live in a big house in Walderslade if they helped him. Some of them thought they were making a movie. The paramedic said... what was his name again?'

'Jay Jeffries.'

'Yeah him. The paramedic said he was high as a kite on something that wasn't over the counter or medicinal. Anyway, I guess they will be taken back to the station, processed and questioned and if there is nothing to charge them with, they will be released.'

'That's it?' I asked.

'What else is there?' he asked in return.

'They're homeless, man. How about giving them some help?'

He all but laughed at me, 'We're not here to solve the world's problems. Some people are just homeless. Some of them prefer it that way. Some don't know how to live any other way.' He saw my expression and softened, 'Look, they'll at least get a couple of hot meals and some new clothes before they are released.'

I let it go. I knew he was right. Homeless people are an unpleasant fact of life. 'Are we free to go?'

He was putting equipment back into the boot of his car, the torches and other paraphernalia no longer needed as they closed down the scene. He looked across at me, 'I think so. Just wait here a moment while I check, please,' he moved away a pace to use his radio, turning back a few seconds later to confirm no one felt a need to hold us here any longer.

I nodded my thanks. 'Ben, let's go.' Big Ben was twenty yards away chatting to a pretty female police officer. This was usual activity for him, he probably already had her number. She had my dogs in the back of her squad car to keep them warm, something I had insisted the police take care of while further insisting that they had the wrong people in cuffs.

Ben raised a hand to give me a thumbs up without looking my way then ducked his head to nibble on the lady's neck. She ducked away, giggling self-consciously as she glanced around to see who was watching. She said something I didn't hear as she moved to the side of the squad car and let my dogs out. Perhaps confused by all that had been going on tonight, they spotted the reporter lady approaching again and tore off to attack her, slipping through Big Ben's attempt to stop them.

This time, when I yelled, they stopped and looked my way. 'This way, please chaps.' I insisted and got on my knees so they would come to me. The lady followed them, a notebook and pen in her hand and small recording device on a string around her neck. I stood up with a dog under each arm. 'Can I help you?' I asked, not really meaning it, but being polite because that is what one does.

'I'm Sharon Maycroft reporting for the Weald Word. I'm looking for Tempest Michaels,' she replied. 'That's you, isn't it?'

I nodded, wondering where this was leading. Keen to be somewhere else, I asked, 'How can I help you?'

'I just spoke with Richard Claythorn, he says that you rescued him from a gang of men pretending to be werewolves. Can I ask what your profession is please?'

I smiled wryly to myself as I replied, 'Paranormal Investigator.'

The End

Except it isn't. There's another adventure waiting for you as soon as you are ready. Turn the page or click down to see what comes next and explore the offer of FREE stories.

Author Notes:

IF YOU ARE WONDERING why I wrote ten books and then chose to pen an origin story, the answer is because people asked me to. The early books hinted at how the business came into being and the typo that led to Tempest becoming a paranormal investigator. I guess that after teasing people for ten books, the readers decided they wanted more detail.

I caved to peer pressure mostly because it sounded like a fun project.

When I set out to be an author, I had no real idea what I was doing, just a head full of stories I wanted to tell and a bunch of characters waiting to be thrown into an adventure. Were I starting over, this would be book one, not book eleven. Not that I think it really matters, and as I write this note, more than two years after I originally published the story, I can happily state that no one has ever questioned it or complained.

The series is now twenty books deep, the characters developing and changing as we all do. They have enjoyed crossover stories with characters from my other stories and faced more creatures, adventures, and challenges than I could have imagined when I started to pen the very first story. At some point the stories will come to a natural conclusion, for now though, I will nudge you to click down or turn one more page so you can see the next book in this series.

Night Work turned out to be one of the most enjoyable books in this series for me as a writer. Jane Butterworth is such an intriguing character. I am sure you will enjoy her adventure too.

Take care.

Steve Higgs

More Books By Steve Higgs

9 781915 757135